You Never Can Tell

Smog

Books by M.E. Sharpe

Non-Fiction

JOHN KENNETH GALBRAITH AND THE LOWER ECONOMICS

AMERICA IN DECLINE

Fiction and Poetry

THOU SHALT NOT KILL UNLESS OTHERWISE INSTRUCTED

REQUIEM FOR NEW ORLEANS

CANDIDE THE TENTH AND OTHER AGITATIONS

ALL FOR NAUGHT (FORTHCOMING)

You Never Can Tell

Smog

Two Novellas

M.E. Sharpe

Routledge
Taylor & Francis Group

LONDON AND NEW YORK

First published 2013 by M.E. Sharpe

Published 2015 by Routledge
2 Park Square, Milton Park, Abingdon, Oxon OX14 4RN
711 Third Avenue, New York, NY 10017, USA

Routledge is an imprint of the Taylor & Francis Group, an informa business

Sharpe, M. E.
  [Novellas. Selections]
  You Never Can Tell; Smog : Two Novellas / by M.E. Sharpe.
    pages cm
  ISBN 978-0-7656-4069-7 (pbk.)
  I. Sharpe, M. E. Smog. II. Title.

PS3619.H356648Y68 2013
813'.6—dc23   2012041756

ISBN 13: 9780765640697 (pbk)

To my wife Carole, and
my children Susanna, Matthew, Elisabeth, Hana
and in memory of Kenneth Boulding, Alfred Eichner,
John Kenneth Galbraith, Wassily Leontief

Acknowledgments

The best of the best: Angela Piliouras, production editor; Susanna Sharpe, copy editor; Zeph Ernest, graphic arts specialist; Corina Santos, proofreader; Martine Berliet, Julien Simiand, Kimberly Giambattisto, and Irina Burns, translators and transliterators; Liz Dancho, author photographer; Jesse Sanchez, cover and interior designer; Carole Brafman Sharpe, advisor on all matters.

You Never
Can Tell

ᔕ WARNING! ᔐ

Read the Postscript last. I put it last so you would read it last. The Postscript reveals secrets.

Table of Contents

The Trust Fund

"I'll give all the money away!" So exclaimed young Philip Valentine as he sat across the desk from middle-aged Frank McCord, an attorney.

"At the moment, you have no money to give away," replied McCord. "The money is going into a trust fund. You are the sole beneficiary. You cannot touch any of the money until you are twenty-six years old. Then you can touch ten percent of it. You are now twenty-one. When you are thirty-one, you can touch another forty percent. When you are thirty-six, you can touch the balance of fifty percent. If my arithmetic is correct, you have fifteen years to decide whether you will give all the money away. You are an idealistic young man. You think that a great deal of money will corrupt you. Let's see what you think in the course of the next fifteen years."

"My mind is made up. I'll give all the money away." Pause. "Out of curiosity, how much money are we talking about? Who put up the money? Why are they giving it to me?"

"At present, I can't answer any of these questions. In due time you will learn the details, most of them. All I can say now is that we're talking about a substantial sum."

"How do I know that you're not putting me on?"

"I have no reason to put you on. Here is a certified document that repeats everything that I have told you. I am the sole trustee. I have signed the document as an officer of the court. I have no reason to risk disbarment for the sake of a joke."

Frank McCord handed the document to Philip Valentine.

"May I tell my parents?"

"You may tell anyone you like."

Valentine got up from his chair and left McCord's office in a state of disbelief. As he walked down the street of the small New England village where he lived, he tried to make sense of what he had just heard. He had graduated from Cornell University in May. He had sent out applications to several medical schools. He had expected life to unfold along anticipated lines. But would it? His parents owned a small bookstore. They were middle-middle-class, with an income slightly below the median of Seacrest. They were in no position to establish a trust fund. The cost of college was a strain on them. His younger sister Gloria was about to enter college herself. That would put an even greater strain on them.

Philip thought about his relatives. None was in a position to establish a trust fund with a "substantial sum," as McCord had put it. He thought about his college classmates. Some very good friends, some with rich parents, but what was he to them? He particularly liked Dorothea Brooke but she didn't particularly like him. Her family was rich but might as well have been poor, for all it affected him.

Then Philip remembered reading *Great Expectations*. An orphan had been showered with a fortune by a complete stranger for a small favor he had done as a boy. Had he helped some anonymous person in some trivial way that earned the eternal gratitude of somebody he didn't even know? Or at least didn't suspect? His thoughts turned toward people he did not suspect. He had helped customers at his parents' bookstore. He helped them find books they were looking for. He helped arrange signings by visiting authors. He recommended new titles to book groups. When it was raining he held an umbrella over the heads of shoppers as they walked to their cars. He delivered books to the homes of sick customers. Since nearly everybody in Seacrest visited the bookstore from time to time, nearly everybody knew Philip Valentine.

Had he helped someone in some trivial way that earned the eternal gratitude of a visitor he did not even suspect?

Chapter 2

Lakeside Estate

Philip Valentine's college friend George Boot spent summers at his parents' estate in the Berkshires. The estate was situated along a large, placid lake and boasted a magnificent cherry orchard. The sixteen-bedroom house dating from 1900, aside from the usual public rooms, had an indoor pool, an exercise room, a billiard room, and a sauna. Another pool was situated on the lawn to the west of the house, a tennis court to the north, and a tree-shaded amphitheater to the east. It was open house for the entire summer.

All this munificence was the property of Mr. Harold Boot, founder and manager of a hedge fund appropriately named The iBoot Fund, which invested in digital technology in tax-exempt locations throughout the world, headquarters a mailbox in the Cayman Islands. Mrs. Cynthia Boot was a would-be novelist who had a number of works in a drawer awaiting completion.

During the current summer, and during the previous three summers, Philip Valentine had ensconced himself in one of the bedrooms as had a dozen or so friends of George Boot. At the moment, George was a man-about-town with no particular vocation in mind. His younger sister, Dolly, was a law student. Lakeside is a small village of vacationers, so man-about-village might be a better epithet for George. Except that for the rest of the year, he lived in his parents' fifteen-thousand-square-foot penthouse apartment overlooking

Central Park in New York. When in Lakeside, he was a man-about-village. When in New York, he was a man-about-town. In any case, he did nothing wherever he was.

Aside from tennis, swimming, boating, billiards, and flirting, George's guests were not idle. Philip had organized an amateur theater group that put on plays by Shakespeare, Ibsen, Chekhov, Shaw, O'Casey, Miller, and a few others. At the moment, rehearsals were ongoing for *The Taming of the Shrew*, considered a terrible choice by most of the neighbors because of its blatant misogyny. Cynthia Boot was up in arms. Petruchio is a monster. I do not like to see Katharina's spirit crushed. Harold Boot replied it's just a play. You should not take it seriously. Cynthia Boot replied I do take it seriously. Dolly Boot had a part. She did not protest. By the end of June, the cast was ready. Friends and neighbors gathered in the amphitheater. Old lethargic Michael Oblonsky managed to rouse himself from his bed and trudge over from his neighboring estate. At the same time, two young women walked along paths through the woods toward the outdoor theater. Dorothea Brooke in earnest conversation with her scholarly teacher Edward Caslin, and Elizabeth Bennett, alone with her apprehensions. I find the play repugnant. I don't know how I can sit through it, she thought as she took her seat in the amphitheater.

Petruchio was his usual obnoxious self. Kate was her usual obnoxious self. They married. Petruchio continued to be his usual obnoxious self. (You know all this.) Kate then declared:

"Do you see this dagger, Petruchio?" [holding a dagger in her hand.]

Petruchio: "Aye, Kate. 'Tis mine."

Katharina: "Do not dare to sleep lest you awake to find it plunged in your heart."

Petruchio: "Give it to me!"

Katharina: "I will not!"

"Just a minute," called out someone in the audience. "Those lines are not in the play."

"I have adapted the play for modern times." So responded Philip Valentine.

A man in the audience: "You are desecrating Shakespeare."

"That's all right," a woman shouted. "Go ahead and desecrate."

The actors continued.

Katharina: "I will pour a bucket of scalding water on you next time you sleep."

Petruchio: "Please!"

Katharina: "I will put scorpions in your bed."

Petruchio: "Ah, no! Not that!"

"Hold everything," said Harold Boot, as he walked onto the stage. "In those days women were not considered equal to men. You are tampering with Shakespeare's authenticity."

His daughter Dolly, playing Kate's younger sister Bianca: "Hear this out, father, and I think you will be reconciled with what we've done."

The play continued, with Harold Boot standing on the stage, not knowing what to do with his arms, hands, or posture.

Katharina: "If we be equal partners, I will be your loving wife and save you from all harm. Protect and cherish you. These are my honorable terms."

Petruchio: "Kate, you are harsh."

(Boot is walking around the stage, distracting the spectators. "Please sit down, Boot," someone calls out.)

Katharina: "I am not your pet dog. I do not come at your beck and call."

(Boot leaves the stage.)

Petruchio: "I can be kind."

Katharina: "I wish for your kindness."
Petruchio: "Then you shall have it."
Katharina: [To audience]

Do not stab your mate. If he play
A game, with all your wit play it back
And you shall prevail.

Petruchio:

You are a strong woman, Kate.
I do love you.

Katharina:

You are a strong man, Petruchio.
I do love you. [They embrace.]

A voice from backstage: "The shrew is not tamed."
Another voice: "Not so. Husband and wife have tamed each other."
(This is the end of the play. No curtain. We are sitting in an amphitheater.)
Loud applause. Much discussion. The audience is basically pleased. The actors are basically pleased. Philip Valentine is very pleased.

The Bluebird of Happiness

Lanfrey Clandon, a summer guest at Lakeside Estate, spent his spare time writing about New England wildflowers for a new weekly magazine called *Pleasant Times*, paid circulation five-hundred-and-three. He had already covered eastern skunk cabbage, Canada mayflowers, wild sarsaparilla, and the white-fringed orchid. On a lark, he and a few friends had started *Pleasant Times* to report only good news: weddings, parties, graduations, tax abatements—that sort of thing. They reviewed *H. M. S. Pinafore* when it was revived. They wrote about a new paperback edition of *The Thurber Carnival.* They covered soccer games if they did not end in riots.

Clandon and friends, a total of eight to be exact, had sublet a six-by-ten space from an insurance agent whose office on Forty-Second Street overlooked the New York Public Library. After four months of publication, the founders met at their office to discuss the future of *Pleasant Times.* What with a desk, two chairs, and a coat rack, it was standing-room only. Had the city council known, they would have put up a sign saying "Capacity three people." In the crush the meeting was not pleasant. The unpaid stringers were tired of covering wedding and parties, which were covered in the mainstream press anyway. They also felt a bit hypocritical when they realized how much suffering went into preparing weddings and parties. The stringers were ready to quit. Clandon had heard of a national happiness index, which ranked countries according to national happiness. Currently Costa Rica was ranked first. Why not search the world for the happiest places?

"I have friends from Puerto Rico. I can tell you that it's not a happy country," said one of the participants.

"I said Costa Rica, not Puerto Rico," Clandon replied.

"Puerto Rico is an island in the Caribbean. Costa Rica is in Central America. Puerto Rico is a protectorate of the United States, or something like that. Costa Rica is an independent country with no army. You have to admit that's a plus."

"All right, then. But we have no money to send someone to Costa Rica to report on happiness there."

"Not to worry. My friend Bess Semple is going to Costa Rica on a vacation. She has agreed to write an article."

"Sounds good to me. After Costa Rica, we can go right down the list of happiness countries and we'll be in business for a long time. How does the U.S. rank, by the way?"

"We're one-hundred-and-fifty."

"Oh."

Shortly thereafter the meeting broke up.

Shortly thereafter Bess Semple went to Costa Rica on vacation and wrote an article reporting a high level of happiness among American tourists at the five-star beach-front hotels. But in her one incursion into the outskirts of the capital San José, she found poor people living in shacks and did not possess the intestinal fortitude to probe into their level of happiness. Moreover, she did not speak Spanish.

Pleasant Times discontinued publication shortly thereafter.

Meanwhile, Lanfrey Clandon received an email from *Le Monde* in Paris asking him to go to Afghanistan for one month to assess the situation there and write four weekly reports for a fee of fifty-thousand-dollars, all expenses paid.

"I cannot go. I have other responsibilities," he emailed back, although he had no other responsibilities and had no idea why they asked him. His self-respect was far too great to acknowledge that he felt nothing but abject fear at the mere thought of going to Afghanistan.

Le Monde replied, "We understand that you have other responsibilities. We would like to offer you a fee of one-hundred-thousand-dollars."

Clandon emailed back about security problems.

"We will provide an armored Jeep and four security guards. Our fee is one-hundred-and-fifty-thousand-dollars."

Clandon consulted Walter, the manager of Lakeside Estate, a man esteemed for his common sense.

"You never can tell. You could get run over by a bus in New York."

Clandon gathered up his short supply of courage, and emailed back: "I need two-hundred-thousand-dollars for this assignment."

Within an hour a one-word email arrived. "Agreed." He went.

Clandon took the opportunity to write about locoweed, spiney rustharrow, mimosa, wormwood, and poppy cultivation. In other respects, his four reports all said the same thing: The situation is hopeless. He was much relieved to return to New York unscathed. And to receive a check for two-hundred-thousand dollars.

But consternation broke out in the offices of *Le Monde* in Paris.

L'éditeur en chef Mr. Lapidou à son assistant: "Vous avez envoyé le mauvais Lanfrey Clandon en Afghanistan."

"Mais de quoi parlez vous?"

"Lanfrey Clandon est le correspondant de guerre célèbre qui a couvert l'Afghanistan pendant cinq ans et qui a écrit le best-seller *La guerre sans fin*. Vous avez envoyé un inconnu qui porte le même nom."

"Mais ses dépêches étaient si bien écrites!"

"On s'en fout de ses dépêches! Elles n'ont rien à voir avec le vrai Lanfrey Clandon."

"Vous avez raison, Monsieur."

"Alors, on fait quoi maintenant?"

"Je suppose qu'il faut se faire une raison, monsieur, n'en parler à personne, et se remettre au travail."

"Et que va dire le vrai Lanfrey Clandon?"

"Soyons optimistes, Monsieur."

"Vous êtes un imbécile."

Or in other words:

The editor-in-chief M. Lapidou to his assistant: "You have sent the wrong Lanfrey Clandon on the assignment to Afghanistan."

"What are you talking about?"

"Lanfrey Clandon is the famous war correspondent who covered Afghanistan for five years and wrote the bestselling account *The War Without End*. You sent some nobody with the same name."

"But his dispatches were well-written."

"Damn his dispatches. They are not genuine Lanfrey Clandon."

"You have a point, sir."

"What are we to do?"

"I suppose that we must suck it up, sir, say nothing, put on a brave front, and get on with business."

"What will the real Lanfrey Clandon say?"

"Let us hope for the best, sir."

"You are a fool."

Our Lanfrey Clandon was none the wiser. But he did wonder why he was asked to take on such a strange assignment. Perhaps he was better known for his fine writing than he realized. Perhaps his subscription to *Le Monde* had something to do with it. He had studied French in high school, after all.

His vastly different encounters with *Pleasant Times* and *Le Monde* led to a moment of self-reflection. What should he aspire to? As he trolled through the Internet, he came across a song recorded by Jan Peerce long ago. His voice conveyed sorrow, suffering, and hope at the same time.

> *You will find greater peace of mind*
> *Knowing there's a bluebird of happiness.*
> *We are in a world that's just begun . . .*

Clandon thought: Let it come to you lest it fly away.

When he was not engaged in self-reflection, two-hundred-thousand-dollars in the bank gave him a great deal of comfort.

The High Cost of Illusions

Lanfrey Clandon returned to Lakeside Estate after his arduous labors in Afghanistan and was asleep in his bed at ten in the morning dreaming of bluebirds flying around his room. He heard a knock at the door. Walter informed him that a reporter from the *New York Times* had tracked him down and requested an interview. As he dressed, Lanfrey speculated about his fleeting moment of fame. Could he, should he, try to stretch it out into a longer moment, perhaps by writing a book, perhaps by lecturing on campuses, perhaps by founding an organization to aid refugees? Perhaps, perhaps. He could not think clearly so early in the morning. I shall consult Walter, he mused.

At the same time, Dorothea Brooke was making her way to Lakeside Estate through a path in the woods to meet her teacher Edward Caslin. Her parents would not allow her to meet Caslin at home. They did not like him. They did not like him as a friend of their daughter. They did not like the illusions that Dorothea harbored about him. She encountered Cynthia Boot in the breakfast room.

"Sit down and have a cup of tea with me." Cynthia Boot was in her robe and had not showered or made up and the lines in her face and neck stood out.

Dorothea needed confirmation of her intuitions. "I greatly admire Edward Caslin, as you may know."

"Pity," said Cynthia Boot. "I don't know about the great work that you claim he is doing. I do know that you are twenty-two and he is seventy and prematurely aged and a walking cadaver."

Dorothea reddened. "He is doing great work. He is studying modern medicine looking for common elements that could point to more effective treatments of illness."

"Let him. I wish him success. What's that to you?"

"I am helping him. I want my life to be worthwhile. I want to contribute to the great work he is doing. I intend to marry him."

Cynthia Boot dropped her teacup. She and Dorothea mopped up the tablecloth with their napkins.

"Please. The work is dazzling you, not the man."

"Mrs. Boot, he has spent the last twenty years studying modern medicine and is on the verge of finishing his great life work. As his wife, I can help him, encourage him, give him the will to go on."

Dorothea Brooke was seeking a purpose greater than her selfish personal needs. Edward Caslin's work supplied that purpose. She would marry him and help him carry his work to a conclusion, a conclusion that would benefit all mankind. She was in love with Caslin's work. That love was transmuted into love of Caslin, or at least deep respect for him. Yes, he was seventy years old and she was twenty-two. Yes, he was cadaverous in appearance, but she didn't notice, or looked past that at the essence of the man. She would marry him.

Her parents shrank from the thought. Even kindly Walter advised against it. But Dorothea possessed an indomitable will to live for a purpose greater than herself.

She married him.

She helped him with his research. She transcribed his notes onto index cards. She fortified Caslin's sense of self-importance. But he gave nothing back. He was a cold man. He had no kind words to say. The bed was cold. In three months Dorothea recognized her love as an illusion and it died out. If it was love. She soldiered on for another three months. Then Edward Caslin suddenly died of a stroke.

The Brookes, the Boots, and Philip Valentine attended the funeral and gave their solace to dry-eyed Dorothea.

Several weeks later, she looked over Caslin's work. He had accumulated some two-thousand three-by-five cards over the past twenty years. They contained nothing more than a hodge-podge of facts that added up to nothing. Dorothea began to think of other worthy causes. Her ideas were inchoate. It was too soon to make any decisions. She lived from day to day. She did not mourn Edward Caslin. She mourned her lost illusion.

From time to time, Lanfrey Clandon and Dorothea Brooke passed each other in the gardens and paths of Lakeside Estate, one looking ineffably pleased, the other looking ineffably sad. Philip Valentine came up on his vacations from medical school to see Dolly Boot on her vacations.

Philip: "You know, I have a great secret."

Dolly: "If you tell me, it won't be a secret."

Philip: "It will be our secret."

Dolly: "That sounds romantic."

Philip: "Someone gave me a trust fund."

Dolly: "Who?"

Philip: "I don't know."

Dolly: "Why don't you?"

Philip: "The lawyer for the trust fund was instructed to keep the benefactor anonymous."

Dolly: "Who is the lawyer?"

Philip: "Frank McCord."

Dolly: "He's my father's lawyer too."

Philip: "I know."

Dolly: "I'll see if I can get my father to find out who's the benefactor. McCord owes my father a lot."

Philip: "He won't find out. McCord's lips are sealed."

Dolly: "We shall see. Do you have any suspects?"

Philip: "I haven't a clue."

Dolly: "How much money?"

Philip: "Heaps."

Meanwhile, Philip was also welcome at the Brookes' estate. He and Dorothea became better friends. Their mutual goal was to find a purpose in life. It was in their natures.

Chapter 5

An Incident on the Lake

"Wha-d'ya say we go out on the town?" proposed Jim Fenimore, the young handyman at the Lakeside Bar and Grill to Mary Garth, the young waitress.

"Town! Lakeside is not a town. It's hardly a village what with a year-round population short of three-hundred."

"Just a manner of speaking."

Jim Fenimore was a lithe lothario with uncommonly good looks and a head of dark hair that casually fell over his forehead, making other men envious. Mary Garth was a short, somewhat full-bosomed blonde in excellent condition as a result of rigorous daily exercise.

"Where do you propose going?"

"We could drive into Danbury and see a rerun of *Gone with the Wind.*"

"If you promise to buy me popcorn and soda."

"Promise."

Jim really liked Mary. He even had thoughts of marrying Mary. But Mary was a poor local. Together they would remain poor locals, stuck in Lakeside, destined to be handyman and waitress at the Lakeside Bar and Grill forever until death did them part.

What about Dolly Boot, an heiress? The Lakeside Bar and Grill delivered and sometimes the Boots ordered out and Jim delivered, as a result of which he met Dolly Boot.

"How about a stroll in the cherry orchard?"

"Busy now," replied Dolly, thinking the suggestion was cheeky. But he was handsome.

Next delivery: "How about a dunk in the pool?"

"Can't. Busy now." He has some chutzpah, she thought, silently using a word she had picked up from Sam Jacobs, an occasional visitor. But he does have a nice head of hair and nice buns.

Next delivery: "How about taking a stroll through the woods to the amphitheater?"

What the hell, she thought. It's still light out. And I can scream if necessary. So they took a walk.

Next delivery. And the next. And the next. By then they were kind of kissing. But her family knew nothing about it. What the hell. It was a lark. Kind of fun, but nothing serious. Well, he was seriously sexy. Mary Garth knew nothing about it, either.

Jim's head started to fill with delusions of grandeur. Dolly and I are warming up. She really likes me. She will get hot. Love conquers all, including her parents. Or not. Who cares?

But if Dolly finds out about Mary . . .

Oh, my God! I'm finished. Mary will make no end of trouble. I have to break off with Mary. What if Mary won't go peacefully? Oh my God! I'm finished!

I have to think of something.

"Let's take a canoe out on the lake tonight, Mary. There's a full moon. It will be beautiful."

"Sure. Let's do that, lothario."

Out on the lake. Mary: "The moon is beautiful. The lake is silver. What's wrong with you? You look agitated."

"Yeah. I'm thinking about the future. You a waitress. Me a man-of-all-work. Where do we go from here?"

Mary: "Oh, we settle down together. We buy a small house. We grow a garden. We have children. Maybe you learn a trade and get a job in Danbury. I can do seamstressing at home. We'll make do. It's not how much money we have. It's getting satisfaction from our lives."

Jim grabbed an oar, swung it over his head, swung it down toward Mary, giving Mary a split second to dodge toward the left side of the canoe, tipping it over.

"You bastard! You asshole! You bastard! You asshole!" she screamed in the water.

"I can't swim," he screamed back.

"Die, you pig!" she screamed back.

"I can't swim! Please! Please! I can't swim!"

"Die, you pig!" she screamed as she grabbed his manly forelock and began swimming to shore with him in tow.

He lay on the beach in the light of the full moon before the shimmering lake.

"What a damn fool I have been," said Mary Garth to Dolly Boot.

"What a damn fool I have been," replied Dolly Boot to Mary Garth.

Jim Fenimore disappeared somewhere in the wilds of Indiana.

Renata and Harold and Cynthia and Sam and Tom and Rom

The housekeeper, Renata Rice, is both black and white. That is, she is white but she has black ancestry so she is black. She shuttles back and forth between New York and Lakeside with the Boot family. When she is in New York, she is black. When she is in Lakeside, she is white. The simple fact is that she grew up in an extended African American family in New York, which lived in an African American community. No such community exists in Lakeside.

By coincidence, both Renata Rice and Cynthia Boot gave birth to boys within a week of each other. Tom Boot was a last minute baby. Cynthia Boot was of an age when in a few months she could not have conceived. Rom Rice could have had quite a few younger brothers and sisters had Renata Rice been so inclined.

Tom and Rom looked almost identical. Renata took care of them both and couldn't tell them apart. A contributing factor was the happenstance that Harold Boot was the father of both Tom and Rom. Perhaps he knew it. Perhaps Cynthia Boot suspected it. When she was handed a baby to hold in her arms, she didn't know if it was Tom or Rom. Not that she was concerned. She believed the baby was Tom.

A thought crossed Renata's mind. What if I let Tom's mother think that Rom is Tom and Tom is Rom and Rom grows up to be the heir of the Boot fortune intended for

Tom. In her care, both boys would get loving attention. No one would be any the wiser. A kind of rough justice would be meted out. But no. Her relationship with Harold Boot was consensual. Whatever she decided, there could be no justice. Justice was just not in the cards. So one afternoon before too much time had passed, she took Tom and Rom to the hospital where they were born, and asked a maternity nurse to match up the footprints taken at birth with the footprints of the two babies in the carriage that she was pushing. After Tom and Rom were clearly identified, Renata constantly dressed Tom in navy blue and Rom in magenta so that she could tell them apart. Then one day she noticed that Tom had a small mole on his right shoulder and that Rom did not. She was then able to interchange their clothes without the chance of mistaking Tom with Rom or Rom with Tom.

When Tom and Rom were still quite small, a family friend came to visit the Boots at Lakeside Estate. Sam Jacobs was in his mid fifties and had recently divorced. He was still in the state of mind in which he needed to talk about his troubles to anyone who would listen. Cynthia Boot in particular was willing to listen. She herself needed to talk, not about a recent divorce, but about a prospective one. Really about the insuperable price she would have to pay for a prospective one. One night after bedtime, she padded down to Sam Jacob's room to commiserate. Sam commiserated back. Soon they were commiserating in each other's arms under the covers. Before dawn, Cynthia Boot padded back to her room. She passed the old retainer Pierce in the hallway. "Sh," she uttered as she put her finger to her lips. Pierce was a bit addled and thought nothing further about the early morning encounter in the hallway.

Cynthia Boot occasionally saw a psychiatrist when she was in New York. Her psychiatrist was on the cutting edge of psychotherapy and took a new tack at Cynthia Boot's next visit. This new tack got right to the point and often saved a great deal of time. She asked, "What would make you happy?"

"The death of my husband."

The psychiatrist, Gertrude Steinmetz, was taken aback, but true to her beliefs, she tried to maintain unconditional positive regard for her patient.

"Why would his death make you happy?"

"He plays around. He doesn't care for me. He's cold. He's rarely at home."

"You haven't tried to talk with him?"

"He evades talking."

"Short of his death, is there anything else that would make you happy?"

"I suppose if he acquired Alzheimer's and retreated to another mental world away from me, I could be moderately happy."

"Why not just divorce?"

"I signed a prenup. I should lose everything."

Soon the time was up. Happiness therapy had not gotten very far.

Sam Jacobs had brought his friend Julian Treslow with him. Julian had been brought up in an austere household. He saw much warmth in Jewish households that he happened to be acquainted with. A question came up repeatedly in his conversations with Sam.

"How can I become Jewish?"

"Well, you could start by reading *The Joys of Yiddish*. Yiddish has many interesting expressions that will help you think Jewish. For example, the word 'oy' has no equivalent in English. There's oy vey—oh my goodness, what pain! Oy gevalt—oh, how nasty it is! Oy—what a surprise! Oy—how delicious! Oy—what anguish I'm suffering! Oy—do I have regrets! Oy—I'm scared! Oy, there are so many meanings of oy. Oy, it's a pleasure just to think of them."

"Well, I want to become more Jewish than just knowing the meanings of oy."

"You could study for a bar mitzvah."

"I'll think about it."

"You could get circumcised."

"I don't want to become that Jewish."

"You could take up with a nice Jewish woman."

That was Julian Treslow's choice. Sam Jacobs introduced him to the widow Gertrude Himmel. Her Jewish cooking warmed his stomach and his heart. Her hugs warmed everything. He moved in with her. He was well on his way to becoming Jewish.

Cynthia Boot could not move in with Sam Jacobs. She continued to be miserable.

Harold Boot continued to be a hard man and make money.

Tom and Rom continued to flourish under the care of Renata Rice.

Chapter 7

A Play on Words

"Why don't you go out with George Boot? He's asked you three times now."

Elizabeth Bennett's mother addressing Elizabeth Bennett, who is in her early thirties, vacations at her parents' estate several miles north of Lakeside, and is a nuclear physicist.

"George Boot is the ne'er-do-well son of indifferent parents and is not interested in anything except going to parties and getting drunk. I won't waste my time on him."

"You should think of settling down," sighed Elizabeth's mother.

Bill Darcy also noticed Elizabeth Bennett. But the situation was hopeless. He worked at a gas station in the village and was handsome, affable, and courteous. When Elizabeth drove up to get gas, she was put off by the grease on his coveralls and the odor that permeated them. She didn't notice anything else. Nice, but a snob, Bill thought.

Meanwhile Philip Valentine was planning to put on another play at the Boot amphitheater and asked Elizabeth Bennett if she would be willing to try out for a part. Unknown to her, he had also asked Bill Darcy. She had no reason to say no. A cast was assembled and rehearsals began for *The Merchant of Venice*.

Rehearsals went well and by mid-August neighbors and villagers assembled in the amphitheater for an early evening performance.

Several knots of spectators exchanged opinions about the propriety of putting on a play rife with anti-Semitism, commonplace in Shakespeare's time but unacceptable now. Uneasiness pervaded the audience, not the best mood to accompany an evening's entertainment.

Sam Jacobs played the moneylender Shylock; Bill Darcy played Antonio, who agreed to Shylock's demand for a pound of flesh if he failed to pay off the debt by the due date, confident that he could do so; Lanfrey Clandon played Bassanio, lover of Portia and friend for whom Antonio borrowed the money. Elizabeth Bennett played Portia, lover of Bassanio.

As you might suspect, Philip Valentine was not averse to modernizing the play. What could be more just than making Shylock a Christian, Bassanio a Jew, letting Antonio remain Christian, and making Portia a Jew as well.

Consternation broke out in the audience when the changes became evident.

"What are you doing to Shakespeare!" cried out Harold Boot. "Get off my stage."

"No, no!" shouted Dorothea Brooke. "Let them go on."

"We are not idiots!" yelled Dolly Boot. "We can handle it."

Harold Boot rushed to the stage. Bill Darcy, Lanfrey Clandon, and Sam Jacobs pushed him off.

Portia then addressed the Christian Shylock played by the Jew Jacobs:

The quality of mercy is not strain'd.
It droppeth as the gentle rain from heaven
Upon the place beneath. It is twice blest:
It blesseth him that gives and him that takes.

At that moment someone ran across the stage from right to left and someone else ran after him with a gun in his hand. The audience recognized Johnny Shelley, a cousin of Harold Boot, running for his life, and the lethargic Michael Oblonsky, running after him as fast as he ever ran in his life. Offstage a shot was fired. Darcy, Clandon, and Jacobs wrestled the gun from his hand. Shelley had a slight wound in his left shoulder. Valentine ministered to the wound. The audience lingered long into the evening in a double state of shock, part induced by the attempted murder and part induced by the confusion over Christians becoming Jews and Jews becoming Christians. Harold Boot forgave Darcy, Clandon, and Jacobs, who had forced him off the stage, and Philip, who had ministered to Johnny Shelley, grateful to them for preventing a murder from taking place on his property.

We are not done. During rehearsals, Elizabeth Bennett had come to see Bill Darcy without grease and the odor of gasoline about him. He was indeed affable, courteous, and handsome.

"I have just finished reading *The English Patient* by Michael Ondaatje," he mentioned while they were offstage. "Have you read it?"

"No. But I should like to. May I borrow it?"

"Better than that. It would be my pleasure to give you a copy."

Bill Darcy was also sensitive to beauty around him.

"Have you ever noticed peoples' hands when they hold knives and forks? Those hands are like ballerinas in their elegant postures, and no training is necessary. It comes naturally. Isn't that something?"

Elizabeth Bennett felt remorse about her former pride and Bill Darcy felt remorse about his former prejudice.

Chapter 8

The Passing of Michael Oblonsky

Around one in the morning, Philip Valentine drove Michael Oblonsky home and helped him get into bed. Oblonsky drank eight ounces of vodka to calm his nerves and Valentine drove off. Oblonsky's nerves would not be calm. His head was throbbing, his heart was racing, his lungs were huffing from the exertion earlier in the evening. He hardly ever got out of bed much less run across an amphitheater stage with a gun in his hand. In a crisis, Oblonsky summoned his valet, but his valet had gone off to England to visit his mother. He was alone.

"I'm dying. Please help an old man." These words were conveyed through his iPhone to Millie Garth, the nurse who ministered to him. She came right over. By the time she arrived, Oblonsky was dead.

Millie Garth had ministered to Oblonsky for twenty years. A local M.D. had examined Oblonsky, concluded that he was an imaginary invalid, saw that he, the M.D., could be of no use, and recommended nursing care for the imaginary good that it would do the imaginary invalid. Early on, Oblonsky shook violently from chills. Millie Garth, the nurse in question, covered him with blanket after blanket to no avail. In desperation she got under the covers with him as a last resort to warm up his body with hers and stop the violent chills. This maneuver worked. He warmed up more than she expected and in nine months Mary Garth was born. Oblonsky denied that he had anything to do with it, but agreed to make a cash payment to Millie Garth until Mary Garth finished high school, in addition to Millie Garth's normal nursing fee. Millie Garth became a virtual indentured servant for eighteen years. Meanwhile she became Johnny Shelley's companion.

Well, Oblonsky was definitely dead. Did the lethargic Oblonsky write a will, or did he put it off until tomorrow? The logical place to check was his filing cabinet. Millie took the key from his desk drawer, opened the cabinet, and under "W" found a folder marked "Will."

"Well I'll be damned!" Oblonsky's wretched cousin Jim Fenimore was named the sole heir. The man who had tried to murder Millie's own daughter Mary in a failed attempt to simulate a boating accident on the lake. The sole heir! His own daughter Mary excluded! "I swear I will never let this happen."

On her iPhone to Johnny Shelley: "Oblonsky's dead. Fenimore's getting everything. His own daughter is getting nothing. Get over here before anybody else does so we can decide what to do. "

On arriving, Shelley to Garth: "This is outrageous."
Garth to Shelley: "God must be weeping."
Shelley: "Give me the will." He took a match and burned it to ashes. "Now there is no will."

They talked over what to do and devised a plan.

First they lugged the guts to a freezer in the basement. Then Johnny put on Oblonsky's nightgown and climbed into bed. The bed was surrounded by curtains that could be closed with a cord. He closed them. Then Millie called family members to come quickly. She explained the unusual circumstances. Then she called a notary. "I know it's the middle of the night, but Oblonsky will not live to see daylight. His last wish is to write a will. Please come quickly."

Within an hour the party gathered around the bed. They heard moaning coming from behind the curtains. "Please call a notary." The notary replied: "Be calm. I am here." Women standing around the bed begged, "Please be kind. Please be merciful. Please be generous. Oh, my dear friend."

A voice whispered from behind the curtains. "I give my house and grounds to Johnny Shelley to make up for the wrong I did him. He tried to convince me to remember . . ."

Those gathered around were indignant at the duplicity of Johnny Shelley. To leave the property to himself! Outrageous!

" . . . to remember my daughter Mary Garth. Johnny was right. I hereby leave her all my financial assets."

Consternation in the crowd. "He was worth at least a hundred million beyond the value of the real estate."

"Now give me the will and a pen."

The notary handed the will and the pen to a hand behind the curtain, then the hand behind the curtain handed the will and the pen back to the hand outside the curtain. The name Michael Oblonsky was scribbled at the bottom of the will.

The family members disbursed, grumbling about the self-serving Johnny Shelley but pleased with his gift to Mary Garth.

When Millie and Johnny were alone, Johnny climbed out of bed, got down on his knee before Millie and proposed: "Marry me. Let us own the property jointly." Millie accepted both Johnny and the property. When word got out, the family rejoiced, but still thought Johnny sly.

"Let's lug the guts back up from the freezer and put them back in bed. But we must wait until they return to room temperature before we call the funeral parlor."

So said Johnny Shelley, with Millie Garth in complete agreement.

Chapter 9

Running Away

Mary Garth came into a tremendous amount of money: one-hundred million dollars. She could do anything she pleased. Stop working, buy a mansion, buy a jet plane, travel around the world, join high society. Instead she decided to continue waitressing. She enjoyed it. She met interesting people. She liked the regulars who patronized the Lakeside Bar and Grill. At the same time, she was shocked to find that her father was Oblonsky. Millie Garth had always been evasive. Mary never pressed her on the subject.

A good-looking vacationer named Morris Townsend came in for lunch one day. About forty, friendly, good conversationalist. It came out that he was a lawyer with a practice in New York, very successful, wealthy clients, a litigator, office on Park Avenue. Also very taken with Mary Garth.

"Why don't we go into Danbury on your day off? Untie your apron and we'll go to an upscale restaurant and binge on a bottle of Château Haut-Florin Bordeaux Supérieur 2005."

"Sounds good to me. Pick me up Saturday six p.m. at Fifty-Five Grove Street."

Word had reached Morris Townsend's ear that Mary Garth had come into a great deal of money.

He was certainly enjoyable company and Mary was taken with him. She was falling for him. He became a regular household guest, even accompanied her to the former Oblonsky estate when Mary went to visit her mother, wandered freely around the rooms, examined the books in the library, freely poured himself wine from the decanters, and spread out on the sofa in the study when he wanted to nap.

Millie Garth was suspicious. She was suspicious of every stranger who entered Mary's life after that dramatic night a year ago.

"Test him. Tell him the rumor about the money is just as rumor. You have no money. That's why you're still working as a waitress."

"Oh, mother. He *can't* be false. I can see right through him. I look into his eyes. I see a dear honorable man."

"Then you don't take any risk by testing him."

"You are suspicious beyond words."

Nevertheless, Mary casually mentioned that the money thing was just a rumor, wasn't true, she wouldn't be working as a waitress if it were true.

"It's all the same to me. I love you. I have a good practice. Money doesn't enter into it."

A week later:

"One of my clients has moved to the Bahamas. He's involved in a lawsuit that's going to take a lot of time to straighten out. I'll be away for at least a month." Then he bade a sad goodbye.

Millie Garth went online and found a list of lawyers accredited in New York State. The name Morris Townsend wasn't on the list. Mary was quite aggrieved that she had been lied to, blatantly lied to, and became bitter.

Nonetheless, her aunt Lavinia Pennimore, an occasional visitor to Lakeside village, felt otherwise. She had met Morris Townsend and liked him.

"I don't believe it's the money at all. He was called away on business. He loves you. You have said you see the love in him. I also see the love in him. Please don't make yourself miserable. Keep your heart open to Morris. Maybe he's accredited somewhere else."

Lavinia Pennimore is a woman who recently went through a bitter divorce. At twenty-five she was engaged to be married. An elaborate wedding was planned. On the wedding day, she dressed in her bridal gown, headed for the church in a limousine, when she told the driver, please take me to—and here mentioned a hotel on the West Side of New York, far from the church on the East Side. The wedding party waited and waited. Phone calls were made to no avail. After an hour the wedding party was restless. After two hours they were uneasy. After three hours they were incensed, got up, and walked out of the church. The groom was devastated.

Lavinia fled to the countryside for several months. "I don't really love him," she explained to her mother. "I forced myself to believe that I did."

Her mother conveyed the explanation to family and friends. After a while feelings calmed down, family and friends became philosophical, and Lavinia reappeared. The groom remained bitter.

Then at forty, the drama was repeated. Lavinia could not make a commitment. This time she was forced to flee to Switzerland, where she booked a room at the Hotel D'Angleterre on the shores of Lake Geneva. After weeks of brooding, sitting alone in the solarium and the restaurant, she began to make acquaintances among the guests. A gentleman about twenty years her senior strolled with her, related his life story, at least the part he wished to tell. He was wealthy, divorced, and in need of a wife to manage his home outside London. He made Lavinia a straight business proposition. She was inclined to accept the offer, when one night as she was walking down the hall, saw Frederick, the gentleman, leave the room of a young female guest. That was the end of Lavinia's inclination to accept Frederick's offer.

Overnight she was agitated by thoughts of being forty-five and alone. She had run away before. She would not run away now. She was miserable about stupidly missed opportunities. Not again. She accepted his offer. Not long after, she realized that she had run away when she should have run to the right man and ran to the wrong man when she should have run away. Not many of Lavinia's acquaintances even knew about her hasty marriage followed by her hasty divorce.

Now back at Lakeside, she did not want her niece to miss opportunities as she had. "Marry him. Forget about the money."

But Mary Garth thought otherwise. What love was there? Word had reached Morris Townsend, wherever he was, that Mary Garth had really come into a great deal of money. Word had reached Mary Garth that Morris Townsend had found out. He returned to Lakeside, his eyes full of love, and proposed that he and Mary elope. He would come by in a week at midnight, after he had settled some business matters. They would stay overnight at a nearby hotel and see a justice of the peace the next morning.

They embraced.

At the appointed time, Morris Townsend drove up to Fifty-five Grove Street, got out of his car, and knocked at the door. The house was dark. He knocked and knocked. He pounded the door with his fists. He shouted, "Mary, Mary! Mary, Mary!" And again, "Mary, Mary!"

Chapter 10

Matters Seen in a Different Light

How did Oblonsky get that way? In going over Oblonsky's worldly goods, Millie Garth came across a family album with photographs and biographical notes. His grandparents were members of the Russian nobility. As power was shifting to the Bolsheviks in 1917, they decided to leave before it was too late. They converted all their assets into diamonds and sewed batches of them into their clothes. They took a steamer across the Gulf of Finland from St. Petersburg to Helsinki. They made four hazardous trips, each time carrying diamonds sewn into their clothes, each time secured in a safe deposit box at the Finnish National Bank. Their last trip occurred on October 31, a week before the Bolshevik Revolution. They traveled to London and then to New York. Michael's parents met in New York, where he was born. The Oblonsky family moved in aristocratic circles of expatriates. All this Millie gleaned from the family album.

Michael was a pampered child, an only child, and nothing was required of him.

Then Millie found a diary kept by Michael with only twelve entries made in the summer of 1975. The diary reveals a close friendship between him and a boyhood companion named Lensky prior to that summer. Then a bitter dispute arises. They both fall in love with a young woman named Olga. Olga falls in love with Lensky. Michael is devastated, desolate, lost.

"How can I live without Olga? I cannot. I cannot. I have suffered a fatal wound."

A love letter to Olga says goodbye. He quotes a passage from Eugene Onegin:

Kuda, kuda, kuda vy udalilis
Vesny moei zlatye dni?
Where have you gone,
Oh golden days of my spring?

Michael and Lensky are insanely drawn into a duel. Lensky lives and Oblonsky dies—dies within. Before the duel, Oblonsky attempts to kill himself with the pistol that he intended to use in the duel. He suffers a grave wound to his head but survives. He is never the same again, in body or spirit. He becomes bedridden, a recluse, a misanthrope. His body survived but his soul died.

The letter to Olga was never sent. It remained within the pages of the diary along with a faded picture of Michael and Lensky with Olga standing between them.

Millie and Molly saw Oblonsky in a different light. Not to forgive, but to understand.

Chapter 11

The Romantic

D.J. had two great faults. He was constantly bragging about his irresistibility to women and he was constantly quoting somebody or other. He was muscular, had an infectious smile, and a gravitational pull. Among those who felt his gravitational pull was Dolly Boot. When he visited Lakeside Estate, they played together—tennis, pool, and in the pool. His parents said, go see the world before you settle down. So he traveled.

"The women attacked me in Madrid," he said to Dolly Boot. "What could I do? As Oscar Wilde said, 'The only way to get rid of temptation is to yield to it.'"

"A woman was coming on to me in Moscow, and I quoted Groucho Marx: 'I never forget a face, but in your case I'll make an exception.' Her English wasn't very good and she thought I said let's go to bed. Or maybe she was just pretending to misunderstand."

When speaking about himself and Dolly Boot, he changed his tune. "As James Thurber said," he said to Dolly Boot, "'I love the idea of there being two sexes, don't you?'"

When D. J. contemplated politics, he said: "As Will Rogers put it, 'Politics has become so expensive that it takes a lot of money even to be defeated.'"

"Why do you always comment on everything with a facetious remark?"

"'Humor is a way of holding off how awful life can be, to protect yourself.' Kurt Vonnegut."

"Why do you say life is so awful?"

"Look around you."

"Getting back to your other shortcoming," Dolly Boot rebukes D.J., "Pretend that I'm attacking you. Let's see what happens."

He is at a loss for words, even quoted words. He is evasive. He is shown to be an out and out braggart. "You are not a Don Giovanni, then? Not even a passive Don Giovanni assailed by women?"

What could he say? He was not ready to reveal the fact that he had been frightened by the advances of an adult woman when he was still a pre-pubescent child. When he became post-pubescent he reacted to this event with bravado.

So Dolly bought a copy of *The Joy of Sex* and they studied it together. Dolly had read in the *New York Times* that the Cubans had the most open, most explicit, most uninhibited attitude in the world toward sex, imposed by the Cuban government, starting with graphic sex education in kindergarten.

"Let's go," said Dolly.

D.J. consulted Walter. "You never know," he said knowingly.

They went to Cuba and took a course called "Remedial Sex Education for Adults." All the students were from the United States.

They graduated with high honors and the rest is history.

Chapter 12

Ambassador to the World

Don Quillar is a tall wiry man in his upper seventies, another neighbor of the Boots. He is widely known as Ambassador Quillar, although nobody knows from where or to where he was ambassador. Being known as Ambassador opens many doors.

He is assisted by José Panza, who makes all the arrangements for TV interviews, meetings with bankers and heads of state, and speeches at mass rallies.

On *Meet the Press*, Ambassador Quillar answers a question about the wind farms located in the Texas Panhandle.

"I saw the windmills and advised T. Boone Pickens to build more. They are so beautiful. Then he switched to natural gas. That was a mistake. There's no beauty in natural gas. Windmills are better."

Chris Matthews asked him about his speech at Independence Square in Cairo.

"I told the crowd to throw out Mubarak and start all over again. They followed my advice and did."

José Panza made arrangements for Ambassador Quillar to meet the boy leader of North Korea.

"It is not a good idea to develop atomic weapons."

"No atomic weapons. Just games."

He marched his troops up the hill and down again in Pyongyang.

"No harm. Good exercise for soldiers."

Ambassador Quillar left satisfied with the good intentions of the boy leader.

Ambassador Quillar testified before various congressional committees on subjects about which he was an expert, such as banking regulations, military procurement, states' rights, national parks, and digital photography. Committee members are always pleased to hear expert testimony.

A friend of the Ambassador had tickets to a White House ball but was indisposed. "Why don't you take my tickets?"

"I shall be delighted."

"Where is my beautiful Dulcinea?" he asked José Panza. "I shall take her along."

"She is on a business trip to Hong Kong."

"Ask her to hurry home so we can go to the White House ball together."

Dulcinea came rushing back.

At the White House gate, Ambassador Quillar presented his friend's invitations, but the Secret Service detail didn't bother to look at them.

"Ambassador Quillar, Señora Dulcinea, so good to see you again. Go right in."

Dulcinea, dressed in an exquisite blue gown enhanced by a dazzling diamond necklace, and Don Quillar, dressed in a handsome black tuxedo with a red sash across it, walked regally along the reception line.

"More hot oatmeal at breakfast to keep children's weight down," he said to the First Lady.

"My very thought, Mr. Ambassador," she replied.

To the President he said, "More speed chess for the children to sharpen their minds."

"My very thought, Mr. Ambassador," he replied.

José Panza is quite blunt with Don Quillar. "You can't accomplish anything alone with these crazy appearances. You don't know how to organize anything."

Don Quillar is quite hurt by these words.

Dulcinea consoles him. "Go back to sleep," she says.

"Were these real encounters or did I just imagine them?" he asks.

"Does it matter?" Dulcinea asks back. "Is it any less true if you imagined them? Are they any less consequential?"

Chapter 13

Harold Boot Goes to Washington

Harold Boot invited Elias Filch, a member of the Senate Finance Committee, to visit Lakeside Estate for a discussion of the pending budget bill.

"Section 70F would seriously damage the operations of multinational banks and businesses," said Boot to Filch. He then outlined the problem and suggested that the Senate Finance Committee hold closed-door hearings. Senator Filch was in complete agreement. He returned to Washington and convinced the committee chairman Tom Towers to hold the hearings. Boot had dropped a hint that he would like to help members of the committee get re-elected with contributions from his super PAC. It turned out that Boot was the only witness.

"Distinguished members of the Senate Finance Committee: It's a pleasure to be here again to testify on a matter concerning the health of the entire American economy.

"As you know, Section 70F of the current bill would require American banks and businesses to pay a minimum tax of twenty percent on foreign earnings not repatriated in the current fiscal year. The tax would have to be paid for the year in which the earnings were made.

"The hardship for several thousand American companies that do business abroad would be staggering. The intricate changes in bookkeeping procedures would take years to complete. If the Justice Department sued every major company for missing the filing deadline, the legal system would be clogged with cases for years to come.

"Moreover, the tax would put American firms at a distinct disadvantage in competition with foreign firms not burdened by such a stringent requirement. The loss in American jobs and the setback of the American economy would be incalculable. I see nothing but stagnation for years to come. We would lose at least ten year's growth.

"This section of the bill is also discriminatory. Most individuals and small firms do not invest abroad. While the tax on multinational companies would go up, the tax on those who do not invest abroad would stay the same. This is truly an unfair proposition.

"Then too, we should consider the effect on foreign economies. Any measure that discourages investment abroad harms foreign countries as well as our own. A great deal of foreign development depends on investment in modern technology by American firms. Do we want to harm our foreign neighbors? Of course not. The immediate effect of the contemplated tax would put a brake on the entire international economy.

"I'm confident that the members of the committee do not want to be responsible for causing such grave harm to working people and small businesses in the United States and around the world.

"Senators, take out that provision."

By the end of the testimony, not a single member of the committee had any doubt about the harmful effect of the provision in question. It was taken out of the bill. Only a one-hour hearing was necessary. Not a single person outside the committee chambers knew about the inclusion of the provision followed by its exclusion. Appropriations bills are quite lengthy and complex. No one reads them.

Word had gotten around that Harold Boot was prepared to spend a substantial amount of his super PAC money on the re-election of the members of the Senate Finance Committee. This fact had nothing to do with the decision of the committee members to remove the offending provision. They had been persuaded by Boot's presentation of the facts.

A letter of thanks from Senator Elias Filch addressed to Harold Boot was mailed the following day. Thanks for saving the nation a great deal of unnecessary hardship.

Chapter 14

Gains and Losses

Four years later Philip Valentine graduated from Columbia University School of Medicine and as a resident in pediatrics at Bellevue Hospital saw every childhood disease created since humans walked the earth. Dorothea Brooke is two years behind him. She still aspires to live for a purpose, a realistic purpose now instead of a fantasy.

During these four years, Harold Boot experienced early onset Alzheimer's. The first signs appeared as he started to make ruinous investment decisions resulting in catastrophic losses. His clients fled overnight and the iBoot Fund withered away to nothing. Cynthia Boot became apoplectic with anxiety. Harold Boot changed from a fanatical banker to a blandly smiling patient wandering around Lakeside mansion speaking to himself and others with equal affability. He forgot that Cynthia Boot was his wife and greeted her with the comment, "I have a wife," as though it were someone else. Then he forgot that George Boot was his son, greeting him with the observation, "I have a son." The last person he recognized was Dolly Boot. Then he forgot who she was.

Early on Cynthia, George, and Dolly had a meeting with Frank McCord.

McCord: "We shall have to get him declared incompetent and arrange for you, Mrs. Boot, to exercise the power of attorney over the family's financial affairs."

"I know nothing about financial affairs. We have no financial affairs because we have no money."

"You have financial affairs *because* you have no money. I'm sorry to say that there's no way out except to sell Lakeside Estate and the apartment in New York. I will help you make the arrangements to put them on the market."

Cynthia Boot thought about the manuscripts in her desk drawer, the unfinished novels. Perhaps she could finish them and . . . Her thoughts trailed off into nothingness as she was overtaken by despair. She was unable to think anything, plan anything, or do anything, except dwell on her grim future. In a matter of weeks she too was declared incompetent and the power of attorney was passed on to Dolly Boot, who had recently received her law degree and faced what had to be done with a clear mind.

She put the penthouse apartment on the market and in a matter of months found a buyer. At the same time, she found a buyer for Lakeside Estate, but recoiled at the prospect of selling it to this particular buyer.

This particular buyer was a diversified agribusiness corporation.

"Think how advantageous it would be to have a meat-packing plant in New England," the CEO explained to the board. "We need a distribution center there."

The company hired an architectural firm to draw up plans. The mansion would be converted into corporate offices. The cherry orchard would be chopped down to make room for the processing plant.

All the Boots recoiled at the thought. In particular, George Boot recoiled at the thought. He had tired of being a man-about-town and had taken a degree in environmental engineering. In addition to all the other outrages, he recoiled at the prospect of polluting the lake. When news leaked out, the whole village recoiled at the prospect.

And the prospect of cutting down the cherry orchard. Everyone who had ever seen or heard of the cherry orchard was in despair.

Frank McCord above all else was a realist. "If you don't sell Lakeside Estate, you will not be able to pay for its upkeep. No other buyers have come forth. You have no choice."

Cynthia Boot agonized over her future. The apartment gone. The estate gone. How would she live? She began thinking about selling the furniture, the antiques, the paintings. She wandered around the mansion grieving. "Everything lost. Everything lost."

Philip Valentine was thinking very hard. He was now twenty-six years old. He had been promised ten percent of the trust fund when he reached twenty-six. But ten percent of what? He met with McCord.

"You know what I'm thinking? If I had enough money, I would buy Lakeside Estate and let the Boots continue to live there. I would save the cherry orchard. I would keep everything as it is. Five years ago I was foolish to say that I would give all the money away. But how much money are we talking about? The meat packers offered twenty million. I feel helpless. Nobody is going to give me twenty million. By the way, who is 'nobody'? Nobody must be somebody, and I still don't have a clue about who that might be."

"Look. I can't tell you. But I will transfer ten percent of the trust fund to you as stipulated by the trust agreement."

Frank McCord drove back to Seacrest to make arrangements with the benefactor to transfer ten percent of the trust fund to Philip Valentine.

"Valentine wants to save Lakeside Estate for the benefit of the family that lives there." McCord explains the details to the benefactor.

"The young man has made a wise and just decision," the benefactor observed. "He shows great maturity and generosity for his age. I no longer see the need to parcel out the trust fund in installments, hoping that Philip would use the money wisely and justly as he matured. I am prepared to turn over the entire fund to him now."

McCord was astonished, but not completely astonished because he knew the benefactor and the recipient well enough to understand their respective decisions.

He drove back to Lakeside Estate, sat down with Philip Valentine, and said, "I have been authorized to tell you that the entire amount in the trust fund is one-hundred-and-fifty million dollars."

"I am stunned beyond belief. I don't know anybody who has that kind of money except maybe some of the wealthy neighbors of the Boots here in Lakeview, and they have their own families to look after. Who is the benefactor? Is he or she in his or her right mind? Is it a relative that my parents never told me about? You're driving me crazy!"

"Sorry, Philip. Perhaps with time you will come to realize that life takes some strange turns not to be accounted for. You will gradually come to accept your good fortune without truly understanding it."

"Perhaps you will cheat a little some day and come clean about all this. So we're talking about ten percent of one-hundred-and-fifty million dollars, which comes to fifteen million. One hell of a lot of money. But the meat packers have offered twenty million for Lakeside Estate. So even with a fabulous amount of money showered on me from nowhere, I am still helpless."

"I'm not finished," McCord replies. "Your benefactor is impressed with your wisdom, your sense of justice, and your maturity at the tender age of twenty-six. Your benefactor no longer sees any need to parcel out the trust fund over a period of years, hoping that you would become mature enough not to squander it. I have a bank check made out to you for one-hundred-and-fifty million dollars."

Philip got up from his chair and walked around the sitting room for ten minutes in complete silence, trying to comprehend the meaning of his radical change in fortune. This was not the kind of change in fortune that could be comprehended in ten minutes, ten hours, ten days, ten weeks, or ten months. "I am indebted to someone beyond money." Then his thoughts turned to practical matters.

"The meat company has offered twenty million dollars for the property. Please inform the real estate broker that I offer twenty-one million."

A bidding war followed. The meatpacking conglomerate stopped bidding at twenty-four million. Philip then bid twenty-five million and bought Lakeside Estate.

These negotiations took place so quickly that the Boots knew nothing about them. They wandered around the mansion like lost souls, thinking that the sale to the agribusiness was all but a done deal. They started packing and preparing to leave. In the midst of all the packing Cynthia Boot heard the sound of power saws. "They're cutting down the cherry trees already. Can't they be decent enough to wait until we leave?" She uttered these words to nobody in particular.

In fact the ground crew was cutting down dead trees on the property, cutting branches into logs, and transporting them to a large woodshed. No one realized that Pierce was in the shed piling the logs into stacks. After the logs were transported to the shed, the ground crew foreman locked the shed door. Pierce banged and banged on the door. No one heard him. He crumpled down on the floor and muttered to himself, "Oh well. I'm old and tired. Just as leave die here. Nowhere else to go anyway. Meat company? Bah! They might as well turn me into sausages and sell me over the counter." Then he fell asleep.

"Where's Pierce? Where's Pierce? I need him to move some of the heavy things," shouted Cynthia Boot.

Walter walked around calling "Pierce! Pierce!" but could find him nowhere.

The next morning wood was needed for the kitchen hearth. Walter went to the shed to fetch some logs and returned to the house with a full cart and Pierce sitting on top, blinking from the bright light and doubtful that he was still alive.

By then the Boots heard the news that Philip Valentine had bought Lakeview Estate. The relief was palpable. But then what? They would still have to move out.

Philip sat down with the Boots and made them his proposition.

"You have all been kind to me. I want to return the favor. You may continue to live here as long as you like. I will pay the maintenance for the upkeep of the house and the grounds and the preservation of the cherry orchard. I will put a stipulation in the deed to the property that all successive owners commit to using the house only as a residence and preserving the cherry orchard in perpetuity."

The Boots had difficulty comprehending this radical change of fortune. Why is Philip Valentine doing something out of all proportion to anything we have done for him? Is he doing this to save the estate? Is he doing this to preserve Lakeside village as a peaceful resort? Is he doing this because he wants the estate himself?

After a time George and Dolly came to similar conclusions about themselves. I will visit mother here, but I have my own career. No matter what, I can handle this.

Cynthia Boot's thoughts were not so clear. Now I am beholden to him. But I am no longer beholden to Harold. I am relieved. No, I am bitter. I am poor. No, I am not poor. I still live at Lakeside Estate. But I no longer live in New York. I will be pitied. No, I will be envied. She went on and on and on, miserable, thinking inchoate thoughts. But in a moment of clarity she mused, Heavens, I have a lot to write about. Then she resumed thinking incoherently. I could give all this up and depend on myself. No I couldn't. Perhaps I could . . .

Chapter 15

A Status Report

Do you wonder what happened to the other Lakeside Estate residents and visitors that we have not accounted for?

D.J. becomes a novelist after which he begins to quote himself. Dolly Boot convinces him to marry her.

Julian Treslow is bar mitzvah'd and recites brachas as occasion demands and continues to live with Gertrude Himmel who is an atheist but puts up with Julian's brachas because she is a tolerant atheist.

Elizabeth Bennett and Bill Darcy go their separate ways in the natural course of events and perhaps because of insuperable class differences.

Sam Jacobs and Cynthia Boot share a bedroom at Lakeside Estate and Cynthia Boot stops seeing her psychiatrist.

Tom and Rom play together and are bused to a public school ten miles away where they are learning to sing "You Can't Take That Away from Me."

Renata Rice looks after Tom and Rom, and bathes Harold Boot daily, helping him dress, undress, eat, and change his Depends.

Philip Valentine buys his parents a luxurious condo in Boca Raton and hires a manager to run the bookstore. He repays them the expense of putting himself and his sister Gloria through college.

Dorothea Brooke and Philip Valentine grow in mutual respect and, who knows, maybe they marry some day.

Chapter 16

About the Benefactor

Do you want to learn something about the benefactor whom nobody knows anything about except Frank McCord?

She is an elderly African American woman who lives in a modest house in Seacrest and worked as a maid when she was younger. She visited the bookstore from time to time trying to make up for the fact that she had never graduated from high school. Philip Valentine recommended books to read. He opened her life to literature, to a whole world previously unknown to her. On Philip's recommendation she read Jane Austin and George Eliot. She read Leo Tolstoy and Anton Chekhov. She read Emily Dickinson and Walt Whitman. She read Miguel de Cervantes and William Shakespeare. She read Toni Morrison and Alice Walker. She read Theodore Dreiser and Philip Roth. She read James Baldwin and Ralph Ellison. And many more.

After the transfer of funds, she wrote: "I didn't have a chance to go to college. You are my teacher, my inspiration, my college. You opened a whole world to me." Not signed. Not delivered.

Do you want to know how this working woman acquired so much money?

She took a bus to New York to buy a dress and shoes and to travel around Manhattan in a sightseeing boat. She returned to the bus terminal to store the dress and shoes in a locker before taking the cruise. She found a large unaddressed envelope in the locker. She put her purchases in the locker, inserted the coins, locked the locker, and took the key. When she returned to the bus terminal she took the envelope to the business counter to inquire if anybody had claimed an unaddressed envelope. No one had.

She then consulted Frank McCord. "I advise you to advertise in local papers for two months. List my phone number to call."

No one called.

"Since no one claimed the envelope, I believe that it's yours, for whatever that's worth." So she opened the envelope.

"My Lord! What are these certificates?"

McCord examined them.

"My Lord! They are bonds issued by the National Bank of Switzerland. Let me see how much they are worth."

"My Lord! You have two-hundred million dollars' worth of Swiss government bonds with no name attached to them. My Lord! They can be redeemed upon submission by the bearer. My Lord!"

They both sat in shock.

"It sounds like foul play here," she surmised. "A robbery, a murder, a payoff. God knows what. Somebody just put the envelope in the locker and keeled over dead? A bitter divorce and one side got rid of the money for spite? A totally innocent case of amnesia? The act of someone demented?"

"We'll never know."

"What shall I do? What shall I do? I'm too old to do any good deeds. Maybe I'll give part to charity. Maybe I'll keep part for myself. Maybe I'll give the rest to the boy who opened the world to me. Can you tell me how to do these things? This world certainly is a peculiar place, isn't it?"

* * *

After all this, Frank McCord's lips were sealed. Although he was sorely tempted to unseal them. Perhaps some day he would give in to temptation.

When Philip asked Walter if he thought that the identity of the benefactor would ever be revealed, he replied, "You never can tell. You never can tell."

Postscript

You now know that I have played with well-known plots by well-known authors, turning most of the endings into the opposite of the originals. I can think of two exceptions, which I will come to. If I must provide myself a motive, it is to elucidate the improbability of events, from the most improbable—that we are here in the first place—to the mundane, that any two people will meet, and what will come of it. Borrowing plots is a commonplace practice among writers of fiction, usually not acknowledged. After the primitive stories of each region of the world appeared, very few works of fiction have been wholly original, if any. But to borrow a different story for each chapter, that is brash, and difficult to stop once it is started. A serious purpose lurks in the background. The happy and unhappy endings are ours, and within limits of time and place, we have the power to do something about them. The fate of the cherry orchard is symbolic. Will we or won't we wake up in time to rescue what we deem to be good, valuable, and necessary for our sense of well-being?

In case you missed anything, here are clues to the chapters.

The Trust Fund. As in *Great Expectations*, a young man receives a gift that changes his life. But in this case, he does not find out who bestowed the gift. The young man is Phillip, after Dickens' Phillip or Pip.

Lakeside Estate. The very wealthy Harold Boot presides over his summer residence together with his indecisive wife, Cynthia Boot. As in Chekhov's *The Cherry Orchard*, the feckless wife is unable to come to her senses to save the cherry orchard from destruction. But unlike the original, someone else comes to the rescue. Probably a matter of unreasonable optimism on my part. (All this occurs in a later chapter.) Along the way, I have brought *The Taming of the Shrew* up to date by purging its misogyny.

The Bluebird of Happiness. Taken from *Scoop* by Evelyn Waugh, except in *Scoop*, the well-known war correspondent is rewarded instead of the unknown who happens to have the same name. In this chapter, the amiable estate manager, Walter, makes his appearance. He is well known for his comment, "You never can tell," and he is taken body and soul from Shaw's play, *You Never Can Tell*.

The High Cost of Illusions. In *Middlemarch*, George Elliot describes a young woman of high purpose who deludes herself into marrying a man decades older than she, thinking that she will help him finish his great work, only to find that his work is worthless. In this case, my outcome is the same as that of the original.

An Incident on the Lake. In *An American Tragedy*, Theodore Dreiser describes a young man with aspirations to wealth who drowns his impecunious sweetheart to clear the way to marry an heiress. The drowning is successful, but the hoped-for marriage is thwarted. In my retelling, the scoundrel gets his comeuppance from his impecunious sweetheart.

Renata and Harold and Cynthia and Sam and Tom and Rom. In *Pudd'nhead Wilson*, Mark Twain writes about a fair-skinned black woman who exchanged her newborn son with the son of her slavemaster, with dire consequences. In the case of Tom and Rom, Renata Rice is tempted to exchange the infants, but sees that no good will come of it. A second story in this chapter tells of the Jewish Sam Jacobs, whose Christian friend Julian Treslow wants to become Jewish, as in *The Finkler Question* by Howard Jacobson. A third story about the dalliance between Cynthia Boot and Sam Jacobs harks back to the enmities and infidelities portrayed in Chekhov's plays.

A Play on Words. Again Shakespeare. *The Merchant of Venice* with the anti-Semitism extracted from it. The slothful Michael Oblonsky, taken from *Oblomov* by Ivan Goncharov, makes an appearance. Oblonsky is also a distorted Lensky, taken from *Eugene Onegin* by Alexander Pushkin. He tries to kill Johnny Shelly, or Gianni Schicci, from the opera of the same name by Giacomo Puccini. Yet another story. Elizabeth Bennett is none other than Elizabeth Benet of *Pride and Prejudice* by Jane Austin. But she is rich, and Bill Darcy, originally the wealthy Fitzwilliam Darcy, is poor. In a later chapter, they part company.

The Passing of Michael Oblonsky. We have already established that Oblonsky is a distorted Lensky, a friend of Eugene Onegin. Into the chapter intrudes Millie Garth, transferred from *Gianni Schicci.* The opera here is retold with Johnny Shelley lying in the bed of the dead Oblonsky, who is really Lensky, changing Oblonsky's ill-willed will to a just will.

Running Away. This chapter is derived from *Washington Square* by Henry James. The outcome is the same. The gold-digger is found out by the naïve Mary Garth. I have interpolated the story in *Hotel du Lac* by Anita Brookner. In my version, Lavinia Pennimore runs away from marriage and in the end, marries the wrong man, then divorces him. In *Hotel du Lac,* she is wise enough not to marry the wrong man and remains single and penitent.

Matters Seen in a Different Light. Oblonsky is called Lensky in *Eugene Onegin.* He and his friend Eugene foolishly fight a duel in which Lensky is killed. Tchaikovsky wrote the memorable aria in which Lensky contemplates his death. In the current version, Lensky/Oblonsky attempts to kill himself before the duel and is gravely wounded. This explains his reclusive, misanthropic behavior. As well as the fact that he is a copy of Oblomov, the antihero in the novel by Ivan Goncharov.

The Romantic. D.J. is Don Juan, or Don Giovanni, as in Mozart's opera. Unlike the original Don Juan, he talks about his alleged conquests, but is afraid of women because a woman well into adulthood had frightened him as a child with inappropriate advances. Eventually Dolly Boot cures him.

Ambassador to the World. Don Quillar is a modern Don Quixote, who boasts of great accomplishments and is perhaps recognized as an accomplished man or perhaps not.

Harold Boot Goes to Washington. I myself don't know what novel this chapter derives from.

Gains and Losses. Here we are reminiscing about *The Cherry Orchard,* except that this time the estate is not sold and the cherry orchard is not chopped down. Pierce is the elderly Firs, who is inadvertently boarded up in the abandoned house and left to die. I have saved him.

A Status Report. How things turn out for most of the cast.

About the Benefactor. We find that Phillip Valentine has done a good deed for the benefactor, but unlike Pip in *Great Expectations,* he does not find out who the benefactor is. At least not in this book. I have made a passing reference to *The Importance of Being Ernest* by Oscar Wilde in describing a strange event in a bus terminal, which in Wilde's play, takes place in a train station.

Perhaps this Postscript should never have been written. It has taken great concentration on my part to remember whose plots I have borrowed. Even more so, where the names of the characters originated. Most of them are taken from novels, plays, poems, and operas because they sounded right for the characters, not because they are the names used in the appropriated works. I no longer remember where they were taken from. I suggest that you forget about this Postscript as soon as possible. I hope to do the same.

Smog

Table of Contents

Preface

The title *Smog* is shorthand for our inability to see where we are and where we are going. We suffer from all kinds of extreme weather created by our careless pollution of the atmosphere. We postpone the development of nontoxic wind and solar power until tomorrow. We carelessly pollute our social atmosphere by allowing the allegedly deserving rich to prosper from the want of jobs, homes, and help for the allegedly undeserving poor. We carelessly expend lives on protracted wars that are unwinnable. We allow the upper one-tenth of one percent, even more the upper one-hundredth of one percent, to purchase politicians in both parties as if they were cars in a showroom or items in a jewelry store. We countenance incarceration of minorities . . .

Smog is a play written in the form of a novella in which the presumably knowledgeable affluent members of society are blind to all that is happening around them. They are too preoccupied with their own petty loves, hates, and quarrels to notice.

In 1913, George Bernard Shaw conceived the idea of writing a play about the impending catastrophe toward which all Europe was headed but was ignored by the cultivated, educated upper classes, whose modern Americans counterparts are equally ignorant of impending catastrophe today. His indictment materialized as the hypnotic play *Heartbreak House*, in which the characters go nowhere, accomplish nothing, and pursue their inconsequential pretenses and dalliances as the world crashes around them. Only the aging, prescient Captain Shotover wanders on and off the stage sounding a warning. The ship is headed for the rocks. But no one listens. At the climax of the play, the explosion of bombs dropped from the skies is heard in the distance. In an act of madness, the inhabitants of Heartbreak House turn the lights on instead of off. No stronger metaphor can be imagined for the foolhardiness of the occupants of that fictional but real-life house.

The subtitle of *Heartbreak House* is *A Fantasia in the Russian Manner on English Themes.* In the early twentieth century, three of Chekhov's plays were introduced to the English theatergoing public. The English had never before seen such plays. They are plays of stasis, of mood, of personal bickering and preoccupation, in which in the end very little is resolved. All the while ominous social changes are taking place somewhere in the background, resulting finally in the smashup of world war and revolution, which Chekhov could not foresee. He could see what was in front of him, and it wasn't reassuring.

Shaw was taken with Chekhov's ability to portray the sense of impending doom and the obliviousness and helplessness of his characters before it, which Shaw perceived among the civilized populations of the civilized countries of Europe. As in a Chekhovian play, he wrote a comic tragedy or a tragic comedy. The production of *Heartbreak House* had to be postponed until the war was over. No play of this sort could be performed as war fever gripped England. When the tragedy sank in afterward, the tragedy of *Heartbreak House* sank in as well.

Here we are repeating the same comedy-tragedy in the United States. *Smog* is a novella-play with Chekhov's and Shaw's characters transplanted to our shores and our times.

We have suffered from war delirium and flag waving. We have turned the world over to others to run. Captain Forsyte sounds a warning but is ignored. Professor Milano is incapable of listening. Rich enough to make rash expenditures, but not rich enough to survive disastrous mistakes.

I have ventured to take a step into the future. The truth has become too terrible to bear. The truth must be extinguished. Is this a present truth or a future truth? Is this an act of madness of the present or of the future? We shall have to wait and see.

Chapter 1

The Cast of Characters

Eleanor Chen returned home from a concert tour of the Chen String Quartet, a highly praised ensemble that she founded in 1999. Ms. Chen plays a Guarneri del Gesù, which cost her husband one-and-a-half million dollars. She is forty-seven. Her husband, Victor Milano, retired as professor of American studies at Columbia University when he was sixty-five years old. He is now seventy. The professor owns a large red brick colonial situated on the Long Island Sound in Greenwich. He inherited a fortune from his father who was a banker. The rest of the fortune, aside from the house, is invested in Florida real estate. The professor did not achieve the distinguished career he had hoped for. He is remote, dissatisfied with life, dissatisfied with everything. He and Eleanor Chen have a twelve-year-old child genius, Charles, whom they neglect.

Professor Milano's first wife died fifteen years ago. His late wife's father and two grown children live in a cottage on the Milano property. Captain Forsyte is an ill-tempered eighty-eight-year-old man given to spells of forgetfulness. He became a captain in the Korean War. At the same time he became bitter. Not bitter about himself, but about the villainy of a succession of world leaders and their clueless followers.

Milano's son, Jonathan, is forty and supervises his father's extensive real estate holdings in Florida. He is also a realtor, a vocation for which he has no special interest. He is a skilled cabinetmaker, an avocation for which he does have a special interest. Milano's daughter, Sonya, is thirty-five and regards herself as a failed poet. She has gotten only one slim volume published about animals and flowers.

Doctor Michael Montoya, a specialist in geriatric medicine, is a frequent visitor to the house, originally called to check on the sanity of Captain Forsyte. At age forty-nine he is an ingrained pessimist, or realist as he considers himself. Attorney Eslanda Robinson, an African American, is a knowledgeable lawyer of forty-five, originally an infrequent visitor to the house, visiting when her opinion is needed by Professor Victor Milano. She is a specialist in real estate law. The arrangement of a lawyer visiting a client is unusual, but the fees for her services to Professor Milano make it worthwhile. In fact, her visits have become quite regular.

Chapter 2

A Proposal

Eleanor Chen practices scales in a large enclosed porch at one end of the house. First slowly, then more rapidly, then at stunning speed. As she stops to tune her violin, Dr. Michael Montoya appears at the door.

"May I come in and listen?"

"Please come in. I'm going to take an intermission. I've been practicing for an hour."

"Your scales are breathtaking."

"You are breathtaking."

"Perhaps I am. What brought on this observation at this particular moment?"

"I'm trapped in a horrid marriage with a horrid man."

"Why don't you free yourself?"

"I need the money. I am married to the money. At first I was dazzled by his learning. Then I found out that he had achieved very little. He wrote the definitive biography of John C. Breckenridge. Have you heard of him? He was vice president under James Buchanan and a Confederate general under Robert E. Lee. Have you heard of *John C. Breckenridge and His Times*? A minor book about a minor man. Victor basks in all the glory of a minor scholar. He knows it. That's one reason why he is so ill-humored."

"The money is so important? You have your own distinguished career."

"I cannot live on the scale that I want to, distinguished career or not. I also need love and affection."

She lowered her voice. "Have an affair with me."

He lowered his voice. "How can you make such a proposition?"

"I see you looking at me in a certain way."

"I look at all women in a certain way, most of them."

"Well, act. Life is short."

"Why not Jonathan?"

"Jonathan is temperamental. You are steady."

"Yes. Steady in my cynicism."

Captain Forsyte opened the door to the porch.

"I am interrupting a tête-à-tête. Looks like hormones have been called into play. I will exit and let them play."

He abruptly turned around and left.

Eleanor: "You are a geriatric specialist. It's always doom with him."

"Nothing's wrong with him except old age. He was in a war. What he saw made him bitter."

"Do let's have an affair."

"You certainly can change topics quickly."

Chapter 3

Professor Milano Extends His Holdings

Attorney Eslanda Robinson had an appointment with Professor Victor Milano. She arrived at the scheduled time and rang the bell. No one answered. She rang again. Again no one answered. She rang the bell a third time and then walked into the foyer.

"Is anyone home?" No one answered. She started to walk around the house and encountered Captain Forsyte wandering in the opposite direction.

"Hello, Isabelle," he said.

"My name is not Isabelle. My name is Eslanda."

"I beg your pardon. Forgive me. I am old and forgetful. I am forgetting everything," he said as he wandered off.

Eslanda encountered Jonathan in the parlor and was about to speak when Jonathan ran out, saying over his shoulder, "I am late for an appointment. Do make yourself at home."

On the sun porch, Eslanda encountered Eleanor, who was deeply engrossed in practicing the first violin part of Mozart's String Quartet Number Nineteen in C Major. She was unaware that Eslanda had entered the room.

On her way back to the foyer, Attorney Robinson encountered the housekeeper.

"Doesn't anybody care that I am here?"

"I'm sure that we all care," the woman replied, and turned on the vacuum cleaner, which drowned out all further conversation.

In frustration, Attorney Robinson called Professor Milano on her cell phone. "I am waiting for you in the foyer. No one seems to care that I have arrived."

"Just turn left, walk down the hallway, which leads to my office. You know where it is. I'll be right down."

The substance of the meeting was this. Professor Milano had arranged to buy additional real estate in Florida. He had already obtained mortgages, including a second mortgage on his house in Greenwich, and wished Attorney Robinson to draw up closing papers. The meeting ended with an invitation to stay for dinner.

Everyone was taken aback by Professor Milano's announcement at the dinner table. "I'm investing in another gated community in Vero Beach. I'll rent out the apartments, the usual arrangement. Vacationers like the atmosphere. So I like it too."

Jonathan immediately objected. "You're making a terrible mistake. Housing is way overpriced. At a certain point housing prices will drop like a stone, then stock prices will follow, and you'll be left with nothing. By the way, how are you financing the purchase?"

"None of your business. Well, you're my son and my real estate manager, so I'll tell you anyway. I've taken out mortgages on the Florida property and a second mortgage on this house."

Jonathan: "Even worse. You'll lose money on the gated community and this house as well."

Professor Milano: "I suppose that my investment advisors at J.P.Morgan know more about the housing market than you do. In any case, I'd like you to manage the property."

Jonathan: "You should diversify. Or buy gold. It won't crash."

"Are you going to store the gold in the basement and become a security guard?"

Jonathan sought to recruit some allies.

"Doctor, tell Victor that he's making a terrible mistake. You know he is."

"I'm a guest in this house. It's not my place to intrude into family quarrels. I'd be thrown out."

"Ms. Robinson, you know better. Don't let the professor do such a foolish thing."

"I'm hired as a lawyer, not an advisor. Even so, I wouldn't know what to advise."

"Sonya, speak to our father."

"I don't know anything about business. You know that."

Eleanor looked distressed, but kept silent. She poured herself more coffee as she thought about ways to escape a disaster if it occurred.

Captain Forsyte got up from the table. "We are all living in a house that's rotting at its foundation. Go ahead. Do as you like. You won't save us. Nobody will save us. We are all blind and living in the dark. I know. At least I can see that it's dark." Then he toddled out.

Chapter 4

Sonya's Poem

Sonya is in love with Dr. Michael Montoya. She considers herself plain and ordinary, and has no hope of attracting him.

"Engage him in conversation. See what happens," advises Eleanor Chen.

"I don't want to be rebuffed."

"Then I'll suggest that he take you out to dinner."

"No. Please don't."

Eleanor did casually suggest to Michael that he take Sonya out to dinner. He demurred. Eleanor thought it best to say nothing to Sonya.

The weekend after Professor Milano had thrown his bombshell, the family and friends gathered again. They sat outside on a patio protected from the sun by a large awning. At a lull in the conversation, it occurred to Michael Montoya that he knew nothing about Sonya's work. Why not ask her to recite one of her poems? The request was unprecedented. Sonya was flushed with embarrassment. She had no confidence in her ability to recite a poem nor did she have any confidence to move anyone by any poem that she had written.

Michael Montoya reassured Sonya. "You are among family and friends. Please have mercy on us and recite one of your poems. How could a delightful person like you not write good poems?"

Everyone encouraged Sonya to overcome her fear and coaxed her to recite one of her poems. She made up her mind: I can do it. She stood up and began.

A hundred thousand years passed.
Animals roamed the earth.
Flowers and plants abounded.
Man was nowhere to be seen.
He had sullied his home
and was ashamed.
His numbers diminished
until the human race disappeared.
No humans lived on earth
except Adam and Eve.
Man and woman started over again.
They named the animals, the flowers, the trees.
Bears, dogs, birds, fish.
Spiders, beetles, butterflies, bees.
Roses, daffodils, lilacs, tulips.
Spruce, oak, pine, willow.
The snake bade Eve eat from the tree of knowledge.
She ate. God blessed her.
Adam and Eve multiplied.
Cain and Abel tended sheep, grew grain,
lived side-by-side in peace.
Men and women increased on the face of the earth
and fashioned undreamed of marvels.
A brave new world arose.
Hunger and thirst were unknown.
Wars were unknown.
Hate was unknown.
Suffering was unknown.
Men and women beautified the earth
for a hundred thousand years.

As the sun went down, the listeners sat in silence. After a while a discussion began.

The Professor: "You are done?"

"Yes, I'm done."

Dr. Montoya: "How did you think of that?"

"It's my wish."

Professor: "It won't happen, you know."

Eleanor: "How do you know what will happen?"

Professor: "It won't happen."

Jonathan: "Sonya imagines it. Can't someone think of humans as ultimately good?"

Professor: "Long time in coming. We'll all be dead."

Captain: "Yes, shortly, the way we're headed now. The house is falling in on us and we are too ignorant to notice it. Let Sonya dream her dreams."

Eleanor: "The Captain is right. Let her dream."

Sonya is embarrassed by the discussion. "My poem is a failure. It's too far-fetched. From now on I shall write only about little things."

Dr. Montoya: "No, no. Keep on writing about big things."

Chapter 5

Three Wretched Stories

Sonya began to do public readings, gained confidence in herself, chatted with an increasing number of people, and understood better what her grandfather was talking about. The country was headed toward disaster. She decided to run for Congress.

"Your grandfather was a communist." Eleanor talked straight to Sonya when she heard about her idea of running for Congress.

"I know that."

"You will be pilloried for associating with an ex-communist."

"I can't help what he believed a long time ago."

"It doesn't matter. In politics associations are made that are irrelevant."

"Then nobody can run for office. Everybody has relatives who did something wrong."

"True. Politicians have plenty of mud to sling at each other."

"But Captain Forsyte is a veteran. Veterans are honored."

"Not by their political opponents."

"You say I have lost before I have started."

"That's what I'm saying. Find another way to make a difference. Do you know how the Captain became a communist?"

"I don't know the details."

"I'll tell you," said Eleanor. "He was so bitter about the slaughter that he saw around him that he wanted to clean the slate. Only later did he learn that the communist slate was even dirtier. Then he became embittered with politics. That's why he rants now. I know, because my father was a friend of your grandfather."

"Sit down, Eleanor. Tell me the story."

"Yes. Let's make some tea. We'll sit on the patio and I'll tell you."

"My father came to the United States from China and met your grandfather when they were students. My father closely followed the advance of the so-called Peoples' Liberation Army and was jubilant when they won. But when he returned to China, he was sent to a prison farm to be cleansed of Western ideas. Throughout the ordeal he still believed in the revolution. Without knowing any of this, your grandfather was influenced by my father's intense beliefs. Both men became deeply disillusioned. I came to America to study. Unlike my father, I stayed here. It's still better than China."

Sonya: "Captain Forsyte would dispute that. He is distraught by our drift into chaos."

Michael Montoya walked over. "May I join you? I inadvertently heard some of your conversation."

"Of course. Please sit down."

"My mother also knew Captain Forsyte. For a time they both belonged to the same reading group. My mother was born in Cuba. When she was sixteen, she acted as a courier for Fidel Castro, who was fighting Batista from his bastion in the Sierra Maestro Mountains. When he became the new dictator, my mother and her family emigrated to the United States just in time. They buried jewelry behind their house. My mother will never have the chance to reclaim it. Ironically, I come from one of the richest families in the old Cuba."

"Ironically, I come from one of the richest families in the old China," said Eleanor. "My grandfather was a leading banker."

"My father is not poor," said Sonya. "We are all privileged and still care for others who are not well off. How is that?"

Michael: "It's called conscience."

Sonya: "You have told three wretched stories. Is there no hope?"

Eleanor: "We can look to Gandhi, King, and Aung San Suu Kyi for hope."

Sonya: "My hope is that we don't have to wait a hundred thousand years. So much for running for Congress."

Chapter 6

Fireworks

The lights are out. The patio is dark. A boom is heard intermittently as fireworks go off to celebrate the Fourth of July. Bright colors flash in the sky southward.

"You are all getting drowsy, drowsy. I have put a truth serum in your drinks. You will all speak the truth about your secrets." Eleanor Chen is impersonating a hypnotist.

Jonathan speaks in a drowsy voice. "Something about the dark and the drinks have made us drowsy without your truth serum. The seven of us have drunk seven bottles of wine in two hours. That's truth serum enough to wipe away all our inhibitions. "

Sonya: "Make that six. I don't drink."

The Captain is pacing around the patio carrying a lantern. "What are you going to reveal? You are just running away from reality with your petty loves and hates. My mind is as clear as a bell. I drink to clear my mind."

Dr. Michael Montoya is reclining on a chaise longue. "You are right, Captain. We drink to numb our minds. We don't have the power to do anything about the big problems. We drink so we can talk freely about our little problems." He looked quizzical, then asked: "By the way, why do you carry a lantern instead of a flashlight?"

"Diogenes carried a lantern to find an honest man. I do the same."

Eleanor sits on a sofa alone. "What little problems will my truth serum make you talk about?"

Michael: "I would kiss you right here and now."

The Professor rouses himself with a start. "How can you talk to Eleanor that way?"

"She proposed something of the sort. I am accepting her proposal."

"That is outrageous."

Eleanor rebukes him. "No. It's honest. You paid a large sum of money to a student who claimed you raped her. You paid to keep her quiet. You think I don't know? You don't love me. You just keep up appearances."

The Professor sputters and all he can get out is, "It was consensual."

"If I have an affair with Michael, it will be consensual."

Sonya: "Oh, I can't stand this."

Eleanor: "Do you not love Dr. Montoya? Are you immune to human emotions?"

Sonya runs from the patio.

Dr. Michael Montoya: "I have changed my mind, my feeling, whatever I have changed. I will pursue Sonya."

"What about you, Attorney Robinson?" Eleanor continued with her grilling.

"I'm a lawyer, not a courtesan."

"This is voluntary work. Nobody is getting paid," clarified Eleanor.

"I am not volunteering for anything."

Jonathan blurted out: "Since you have spiked our drinks with your truth serum, I confess, Eleanor. I adore you."

"Everyone seems to adore me."

Attorney Robinson is disturbed. "Why are you doing this, Eleanor? You have upset everyone."

"Why should the truth upset anyone? We are all committed to the truth, aren't we?"

Dr. Montoya: "It's mischievous to tell the truth. We humans can't stand the truth. Let me tell you about the bonobos. They are a species of chimpanzees that live in central Africa. The bonobos solve their problems by making love. They make love to avoid fights. They make love to ease tensions. They make love when they love. They make love with every other bonobo in sight. They don't make war. They don't have unemployment. They don't practice discrimination. Somewhere on the path of evolution, we took a wrong turn. The bonobos are the civilized animals. We are the wild animals."

Jonathan is agitated. "Then let's all take off our clothes and act like bonobos." He begins to take off his clothes.

Dr. Montoya: "Hold it, Jonathan. Keep your pants on. We aren't ready to act like bonobos in public. In public, we're just ready to talk, talk, talk. We'll have to evolve further to act like bonobos. Not far, though. Our genes are ninety-nine percent the same."

Eleanor: "All right, Doctor. You have calmed us all down. We are not bonobos yet."

Sonya returns. "I have changed my mind. I will allow Dr. Montoya to pursue me."

Captain Forsyte has been pacing around the patio lost in his own thoughts. "As Tennyson said, 'The world is too much with us,' by which he meant that we are mired in our petty material interests."

"No, grandfather. It was Wordsworth who said it."

"I am old and forgetful. Let it be Wordsworth who said it. At my age I no longer care who said it. I care about the truth of it."

The fireworks continue to boom intermittently and bright colors flash in the sky.

Chapter 7

An Inspection Trip to Florida

Victor makes an annual inspection tour of his properties in Florida. This year he makes a triumphal return. Property values are booming. His fractional ownership of a NetJets plane allows him to bypass the annoyances at the airport. Eleanor, Jonathan, Sonya, Charles, and the Captain go along for a two-week vacation. Victor has invited Michael as a guest. They stay at the Breakers Hotel in Palm Beach, the most magnificent hotel in Florida. The entry leads into a great hall with frescoed paintings on the ceiling. Each member of the party has a room facing the beach and the ocean. Guests are presented with the daunting task of choosing among eight restaurants offering an entire gamut of world cuisine. The outdoor terraces, pools, manicured lawns, swimming pools, golf and tennis courses, croquet areas, and boating docks satisfy every taste. Worth Avenue, with its dazzling shops, is just a twenty-minute walk.

Victor has concentrated his holdings in Vero Beach, Fort Lauderdale, Naples on the West Coast, and of course Palm Beach. He and Jonathan travel to inspect his property and talk to the local managers. After a week of travel, they return to the Breakers for a week of vacation.

Meanwhile, Michael has been visiting Eleanor in her room.

"I accept your invitation to have an affair."

"How do you know that the invitation still stands?"

"You invited me to your room."

"That was for afternoon tea."

"We could have had tea in the lounge."

"Oh, you are so clever."

Michael leaves, heading to the great dining hall to have dinner with Sonya. At the same time, Jonathan calls Eleanor and suggests they have dinner in her room, a suggestion to which Eleanor agrees.

"I thought we might hang out after dinner."

"We would be committing incest."

"We would only be committing semi-incest. I am your stepson. And we have something in common. We both hate my father."

"Don't kill the goose that laid the golden egg."

Meanwhile, after dinner, Michael suggests that he and Sonya go to his room for a drink.

"You forgot. I don't drink."

"Well, then, we'll find something else to do."

They look out of the bedroom window at the brilliant night sky.

Sonya: "Why are you so cynical?"

Michael: "I'm not cynical. I'm a realist. Enjoy what you can in life."

At the same time, Victor enters the lounge and sees a tall woman in a long black gown sitting at the bar drinking alone.

"Would you like to go to a table and drink together?"

In conversation, they find that they are each estranged from their spouses. They commiserate. Then Eleanor and Jonathan enter the lounge. They sit down at another table after polite introductions are made. A few moments later, Sonya and Michael appear at the lounge entrance. Polite introductions are made all around, and they, too, sit down at another table.

The same evening, Charles is in his room, neglected. He had recently written a paper for science class about the Higgs boson. His father did not understand it or understand why he had written it. Neither did his science teacher. That evening, Charles finds solace talking to Sally on his smartphone. He and Sally are both in sixth grade at a Greenwich elementary school and they are in love.

"You no doubt have noticed that people don't pay attention to the real world any more. They are always busy with their smartphones. Most of the time, anyway. I suppose they still have to brush their teeth and things like that."

"Of course I've noticed. Today I saw, oh, maybe ten mothers and daughters walking down the street each having a conversation with someone else, oblivious of each other."

"Or at dinner, eating like zombies while they are playing games on their smartphones."

"Or in school."

"Or passing an interesting scene in a car without seeing it."

"Or driving a train while texting."

"I've seen pictures of senators tweeting while speeches are being made."

"Don't people want to live real lives any more?"

"Guess not."

When Charles says goodbye to Sally, he still wants company. So he talks to the lady in his phone.

"Lady, what is the meaning of life?"

"You know I'm just a robot and can't answer that question."

"Life has the meaning that we give it."

"Thanks for telling me that. I'll be prepared the next time somebody asks."

"Lady, do you believe in free will or not?"

"Sorry. I can't answer that question."

"Well, let me tell you what Isaac Bashevis Singer said. 'Of course I believe in free will. Do I have a choice?'"

"Thanks for telling me that. I'll be prepared the next time somebody asks. I have free will, then, don't I?"

"No, lady. You are the product of digital algorithms. You are not conscious and therefore have no free will. I am conscious. Consciousness allows me to make choices."

"Oh. Thank you for clearing that up."

The next morning the Captain looks out of his window and sees mud and oil in the water. He sees fish washed up on the beach. He mutters to himself: Global warming. The currents are awry.

Later in the day the company flies back to Connecticut.

Chapter 8

Judgment Day

Eslanda Robinson rang the doorbell. This time Sonya was present and answered it.

"What happened to you?" Sonya blurted out when she saw a cast and sling on Robinson's right arm.

"I was walking down 110th Street in Harlem with a colleague when we saw an angry crowd gathered around several cops who were beating a young black man with their clubs. It was a stop-and-frisk operation. The boy had fallen down on the street and one of the cops had his knee on the boy's back. My colleague shouted that the cop was going to break the boy's spine. Another cop hit my friend squarely on the nose with his baton and he lost his balance and fell back against me, making me fall to the sidewalk. His nose was broken and my arm was broken when I fell."

"I'm so sorry. You were on your way home?"

"No. I live on Park Avenue in the eighties. My colleague and I volunteer to help out on civil rights cases. We were on the way to see a young man we represent. He was seriously injured in another stop-and-frisk incident."

"How do you dress and undress with your arm in a cast?"

"It's not easy. I have a friend who helps me. To change the subject, I'm here to talk to Professor Milano about a business matter."

"You mean about the strange case of lingering smog that descended on one of his gated communities in Florida? It's been a sensational story. I read about it in the paper."

"That's it."

Professor Milano had been stunned when he heard about the problem. He had already been reeling from the harsh words delivered by his wife in the presence of family and friends several weeks earlier. So much so that he started to experience palpitations. Michael Montoya had prescribed a tranquilizer to help relieve the tension. Now Milano was aware that his tenants would not renew their leases in an area with lingering smog. Attorney Robinson stated the obvious. There was nothing to do but write down the value of his assets.

Shortly after the descent of smog on Milano's property, smog began to blight other areas of Florida. A change in wind patterns produced by global warming was carrying polluted air over long distances. Strange storms with intense thunder and lightning accompanied the change in the wind patterns. All of Milano's Florida real estate investments were jeopardized. Then, contrary to his expectations, and contrary to the expectations of his J.P.Morgan consultants, the housing market suddenly collapsed. Milano's assets were wiped out. His debt to banks now greatly exceeded the value of his real estate property. He faced the prospect of having to sell his house in Greenwich. Even worse, it was under water, the colloquial way of saying that the mortgages were greater than the market value of the property.

Two weeks into these financial disasters, Professor Milano didn't appear for breakfast, lunch, or dinner. In the evening, Eleanor Chen opened his door and found him lifeless on the bed. She called 911. An emergency medical team arrived and pronounced Victor Milano dead. The police arrived soon after and began an inquiry into the cause of death. They found a sixteen-ounce glass on his nightstand with milk stains inside the bottom. Next to the glass they found an empty bottle that had contained tranquilizer tablets. The empty glass and the empty bottle were sent off to a forensic lab for examination. The family and the usual visitors to the house were questioned. None of them could shed any light on what had happened. They all agreed that Victor had been deeply depressed.

The technicians at the forensic lab found two sets of fingerprints on the glass: Victor Milano's and Eleanor Chen's. They found three sets of fingerprints on the medicine bottle: Victor Milano's, Eleanor Chen's, and those of the pharmacist. Eleanor Chen became a murder suspect. The family and all the visitors to the house were questioned again. They had all been present when Eleanor Chen had expressed anger at her husband's infidelity and contempt for his mediocrity. But no one said anything about the night on the patio because each one had privately concluded that no one could possibly determine whether Milano had been murdered or had committed suicide. They also knew that the loss of the Florida property and the impending loss of the house in Greenwich had sent Eleanor reeling. Their private conclusions remained the same.

Without anything further to go on, the district attorney saw no substantial grounds to charge Eleanor Chen with murder. The local press wrote about the mysterious circumstances under which Victor Milano died, and the following week moved on to newly breaking news. The local TV anchors did the same.

Michael Montoya, in his capacity as a doctor, spoke to Eleanor about the careless work of the police. If a person swallowed a whole vial of tranquilizers, he would throw them up unless he took an antiemetic. Where is the antiemetic bottle?

Undoubtedly gone with the trash. Where was it bought? Undoubtedly at another pharmacy.

Jonathan Milano brought up another possibility. What if someone had handled the glass and the bottle with disposable gloves? He would leave no fingerprints. Maybe he, Jonathan, had committed the crime.

A funeral was arranged with the immediate family and a few friends in attendance. A light rain was falling. All eyes were dry except Charles's.

Now came the difficult job of moving out and finding another place to live. Jonathan also had to find another way to make a living. He no longer had his father's properties to manage and he no longer had a steady income as a realtor. Housing sales had drastically fallen off. He decided to open a small shop in Greenwich and offer his skills as a cabinetmaker to make furniture repairs. He would rent a small house for himself, Sonya, and the Captain. Eleanor thought about moving to New York, but the problem of practicing in an apartment building to the distress of neighbors convinced her to stay in Greenwich and buy a small house without anticipating a knock on the door from someone trying to take a nap. Sonya thought seriously about writing to make a living, but wondered what she would do before she got anything published. Jonathan assured her that he would provide food and shelter, assuming that he could make a go of the repair shop. In an affluent town, people had money and they had antique furniture, so he was cautiously optimistic.

Montoya and Robinson had seen a disaster in the making and were not surprised when it came to pass. But they would never know whether Milano's death was caused by suicide or murder.

The erratic winds blew smog here and there across America. Global warming was causing drought, wildfires, tornados, and blizzards. The Captain announced: "I have become a follower of Muhammad. He warned us. Worthless leaders will lead us to Judgment Day. We were too busy with our little squabbles to notice."

Chapter 9

Safety First

The papers are full of bad news every day. TV commentators are obsessed with bad news. The news about military failures in Afghanistan and Pakistan has made the United States the object of derision all over the world. The American public has become cynical about everything. Members of the administration and Congress can clearly see that bad news has become a national security issue. The Constitution places the responsibility for national defense in the hands of the president and Congress. Through the secretary of Defense, with the agreement of leaders in Congress, the administration proposes a Safety First Law, which would ban the dissemination and publication of bad news. A Safety First Bill is introduced in Congress, which makes it a crime to report bad news. The bill is supported by both parties and is passed overwhelmingly in the House and Senate; it is signed into law by the president. Since the spreading of bad news is a national security violation, lawbreakers do not have recourse to civilian courts. They are held at Guantánamo and in due course tried by military tribunals. A Safety First Bureau is organized within the Department of Justice.

A case is brought before the Supreme Court. The plaintiffs argue that the Safety First Law is a violation of the constitutional right of free speech. The Court rules, by a vote of five to four, that the constitutional provision for national defense overrides all other considerations. Immediately the press and

TV are forced to suspend reporting bad news since the consequences for doing so are dire. The Reverend Al Sharpton continues to report bad news, attributing unemployment figures
and the like to a hypothetical country that he calls "Country
A." Officials of the Safety First Bureau visit him and advise
that he stop referring to "Country A" since he is using a thinly
disguised ploy, and ask where he got his information from,
since it is now classified.

An underground group of information technology spe-
cialists forms and hacks into the Department of Defense computer system where bad news is downloaded and stored. The
group, which has taken the name Truth First, has designed an
app where smartphone users can secretly gain access to bad
news. The local and state police around the country are depu-
tized to stop and frisk anyone who possesses a smartphone,
black, Latino, or white. The stop-and-frisk procedure is non-
discriminatory. Numerous clashes between the police and
civilians are reported by the Truth First Committee through
their app. Large numbers of blacks, Latinos, and whites are
sent to Guantánamo for detention and in due time military
trial, or to local hospitals.

Eleanor, Jonathan, Sonya, Michael, and Eslanda have
been listening to the Truth First app with increasing alarm.
Eleanor has seen a dictatorship in China and Michael has seen
one in Cuba. Jonathan and Sonya decide to join the underground. Eleanor, Michael, and Eslanda decide to help from the
outside. With great pain, Eleanor sells her Guarneri del Gesù
at auction for two-and-a-half million dollars to raise money
to help the underground. Michael makes himself available to
members who need medical assistance. Eslanda offers legal
counsel to members who have been arrested.

Jonathan and Sonya join a small group whose members
move around from one safe house to another. They frequently

change their email addresses to avoid detection. They set up new websites when their old ones are interdicted. They also use disposable smartphones, which they throw away every few days to avoid tracking. A division of labor is established among the members of the Truth First Committee, rotating the jobs of hacking the Department of Defense computer network and passing on bad news to the public. Eslanda Robinson vainly tries to defend victims of the Safety First Law in court.

Early one morning Sonya is awakened by a knock on the door of the safe house where she is staying. "We have a warrant to search the premises," she hears. There is no way out. A man in his mid-fifties comes in accompanied by a younger man, presumably his assistant. They introduce themselves as officers from the Safety First Bureau. The atmosphere is tense. "Let's sit down and talk," says the older man. "If you want to make yourself some coffee, go ahead. We'll wait."

Sonya feels the need to be polite in return. "Will you have coffee too? I'll make enough for the three of us."

When they are sitting around the kitchen table, the older man speaks. "We have the goods on you. We've been watching what you're doing. You'll end up in Guantánamo."

Sonya listens stoically.

"But we're not going that route. Hey, most of us in the Safety First Bureau use the Truth First app. We want to know what's going on like everybody else. But we can't fight the authorities. We have families that depend on us to pay the rent. My name is Jim Hicks, by the way, and this is Sam Montoya."

"You're not related to Dr. Michael Montoya, are you?"

"Yes, I'm his nephew." Sonya is taken aback.

"Well, let's get on with it," continued Jim Hicks. "We're going to file a report that we didn't find any evidence of illegal activity here. But please, try to be more careful in the future. We're all depending on you Truth First guys."

"Do you mean to say that you're on our side?"

"Yes, that's what I'm saying. And most of the public is too. But we can't do anything about the people running the show. They can always count on a bunch of numbskulls who go around on the streets beating people up who have smartphones in their pockets. Most people leave their smartphones home now. And they definitely have disconnected the GPS so they don't tip off the authorities where the smartphones are hidden."

"You mean the whole country is with us?"

"Almost all. Except the thugs who, you know, make this kind of craziness possible all over the world."

"Do you think that there's any hope that things will turn out well?"

"Who knows? I don't know."

Jim and Sam get up to leave.

Sam has some parting words. "Tell Jonathan, Eleanor, and Michael to be careful."

Jonathan is not so fortunate. A few weeks later he is arrested. No amount of pleading by Eslanda Robinson before a military court can get him released. She promises on his behalf that he will leave the Truth First underground. Eleanor Chen offers to post bail. He is held pending a review by a military appeals court. The next step was to become a non-person in Guantánamo.

Occasionally Sonya comes home. She sits next to her grandfather in the evening under the dark, murky sky on the small porch of the small house. She leans her head on his shoulder and dreams out loud.

"Now I have something to write about and I'm determined to do it."

She pauses. "And I have fallen in love with Sam Montoya and he has fallen in love with me."

At that moment, Charles comes out on the porch in his pajamas. "I have an idea. Why don't you Truth First people go to Canada and blog from there? The Canadians are not going to deport you. They think this whole thing is crazy."

Word spreads. One by one and two by two the Truth First underground moves to Canada. So do the Reverend Al Sharpton and several other TV anchors.

About the Author

Mike Sharpe is founder and president of M.E. Sharpe, Inc., Publisher. He is a trained economist and has expressed the opinion that economics and fiction are usually indistinguishable. Sharpe writes a regular column for *Challenge: The Magazine of Economic Affairs*. He is winner of an Independent Book Publishers Association poetry prize for *Thou Shalt Not Kill Unless Otherwise Instructed*.

www.ingramcontent.com/pod-product-compliance
Ingram Content Group UK Ltd.
Pitfield, Milton Keynes, MK11 3LW, UK
UKHW020427010325
455677UK00029B/1047